# Reflection:
# The Stranger in the Mirror

Records of the Ohanzee Book 1

Rachel R. Smith

# DEDICATION

To my mom, the one who encouraged me to turn
my daydreams into a book in the first place.

# CONTENTS

# PROLOGUE

Darkness threatened to engulf the tiny flame in Argia's lamp as it flickered and sputtered, struggling to remain alight while she and her companion raced through the damp corridor. Only two sounds reached her ears: the echoes of their hasty footsteps bouncing off the surrounding walls and the tranquil lap of the water flowing through the canal. She found herself wishing that her feet would sprout wings and grant them flight. There was no other way she would be able to keep up this speed through the labyrinth of tunnels in the dark underground of Maze.

Valen looked back and squeezed her hand. "Remember, the crime we are committing now is for the good of Renatus in the future," he said with a confident smile, but he did not slow his breakneck pace as he led her onward to their hidden destination.

Although Valen's reassurance was appreciated, it did

nothing to ease Argia's mind. Even the fact that she had already foreseen everything that was about to happen did not alleviate her anxiety. It required all of her focus to avoid slipping on the wet stones and falling into the deep channel just inches away.

Argia had never dreamed she would be in her current situation. Yet, one week ago, it *was* a dream that had led her here. The women in her family were well known for their ability to predict the future. Ever since she was a child, Argia's visions had come to her in the form of dreams which were intensely vivid and startling in their accuracy. But this particular dream was unlike any even *she* had before.

Valen stopped abruptly, and Argia realized they had reached a dead end. She did not need to ask him where they were, for she had already seen what would come next in her dream. With the apparent ease that comes from habit, he reached forward and pushed two seemingly random bricks simultaneously. They slid into the wall with a soft click. A portion of the ceiling above them moved away, and a rope ladder rolled down.

Argia gingerly climbed up, and Valen followed shortly behind, deftly rolling the ladder and closing the hatch behind them. The darkness of the room was oppressive, seeming to close in on the tiny pool of light cast by the guttering lamp in Argia's clammy hands.

"Were you followed?" a woman's voice asked, suddenly shattering the silence.

"Of course not." The words had barely left Valen's mouth when the room was flooded with light, revealing a well-dressed woman with short, graying brown hair standing a few feet away.

"Don't become overly confident. The Gullintanni have eyes everywhere. If they ever learn of our actions..." The woman's stern voice trailed off ominously. Though short in stature, she possessed such a noble air and regal dignity that she seemed to tower over them both. This was the first time that Argia had seen this woman, but based on her demeanor, she must be one of the members of King Gared's council.

"Well, it is safe to speak now. There is no risk of eavesdroppers here," the woman said, her severe expression melting away.

"Who are the Gullintanni?" Argia asked. Judging from the woman's expression, they must be quite formidable. The dream had showed that they would not be caught, regardless of who the Gullintanni were, but she still felt uneasy about breaking the law. She repeated Valen's reassurance from earlier to herself. *The crime I am committing now is for the good of Renatus in the future.*

After a brief pause, the woman looked Argia straight in the eyes and said, "Since you are in this as deeply as we are, you need to know about them. You must never speak of the Gullintanni to anyone outside this room. Their existence is one of our kingdom's most carefully guarded secrets. They are King Gared's personal guardians. They watch over the country from the shadows, ferreting out traitors, reporting governors who abuse their powers, and eliminating threats to the peace. As our current actions go directly against the King's most recent proclamation, I suspect the Gullintanni would consider us to be among those in the first category."

"I understand," Argia replied. She twisted her hands nervously and took a deep breath to compose herself. No matter how accurate she knew her visions to be, there was no way to prepare for actually being in a situation like this. Sometimes her talents were as much a curse as they were a blessing.

A door at the side of the room opened, and the frame was so short that Valen's mentor, Luca, had to duck to step through. In the brief seconds before the door closed, Argia could hear a sputtering hum emanating from the adjoining room.

"Argia, Valen, I am glad to see that you are already here," Luca said. "Are you ready to begin?"

"Yes, almost," the woman replied for them. She turned to Argia. "Valen told us about the details of the prophecy already. He said that the vision was given to you by a woman who appeared in a dream. Can you tell me exactly what the woman said?"

"She didn't actually speak. Instead, she communicated through gestures and revealed to me scenes from the distant future through feelings and impressions of people and places. Her message was a warning of events to come. She showed me the members of your group, and your plans, so that you could include the information from this vision in the same books that you are using to hide the diagrams for your machine," Argia explained.

The tiny woman chewed her lower lip thoughtfully. "It is unnerving that someone would know so much about our plans when we have gone to such lengths to keep them undercover. Your talent is fascinating—and a bit frightening," she said. "What can we do to make sure that the prophecy will be found when it is needed? It will do no good at all if it is discovered after the foretold events have transpired."

"We discussed this already," Valen interjected impatiently.

"I know, but it seems so surreal that I want to hear it from Argia myself," the woman said.

"The dream showed which book will be discovered first and how it will be found. I do not know exactly what date that will be. I only saw the circumstances leading to its discovery and that the events will occur when the time is right," Argia replied.

The woman continued to chew her lip but asked nothing more.

"We need to hurry. The machine isn't going to last much longer," Luca urged.

"First, I have a question of my own," Argia said. "My dream showed me that your plans are to save the books King Gared has decreed should be destroyed. Won't your copies just be found and burned like the rest?"

"No, Gared won't find ours because he is exclusively looking for books related to science and technology," Luca answered. "We are using the machine in the next room to record the information from the books we intend to save onto crystals. The method is a technology from before the Fall of Civilization, and this machine is the last of its kind. Once it breaks, we no longer have the ability to repair it. Unfortunately, you also need it in order to extract the information stored in the crystal. That is why we planned to hide diagrams that show how to build a new one in the covers of six fiction books. Perhaps, one day in the future, someone will be able to recreate the parts needed.

"Your vision will be divided into six sections and hidden inside the covers of the books along with the diagrams. They will be passed down through our families until the one you have foreseen comes. To ensure they do not fall into the wrong hands, we will also program the crystals with your impression of the person described in the prophecy to serve as keys." Luca moved closer and closer to the door as he spoke.

"What do you need me to do?"

Luca opened the door, and Argia could see two more men inside the room. One was hard at work in the corner binding books by hand, and the other tinkered with the source of the mysterious hum—a strange machine connected to six clear crystals. Argia gripped Valen's hand as she followed him into the room and then sat down at the table in front of the machine.

And so the books remained safely hidden, looked upon as precious heirlooms. Their true nature was unknown even to their inherited owners. Despite Argia's terrible vision of the future, the peace of Renatus lasted long after King Gared himself had passed and his great-great-grandchildren were born. They were twins, a boy and a girl, both honorable with great wisdom, admired and respected by all who knew them. Their father continually avoided choosing an heir, unable to decide between two equally worthy candidates. But when the King had grown old, the choice could be delayed no longer. Both heirs became anxious and began to press him, each insisting that they were the one most fit to inherit the throne. So much time had passed and their hopes were so intense that the King could not bear to break the heart of either one by choosing the other. He divided Renatus into two nations, Chiyo and Marise, giving one to each of his beloved children.

The Gullintanni, loyal protectors of the country, were also divided. To avoid either twin feeling that the other was favored with stronger guardians, the group was reassigned arbitrarily using a lottery. These steadfast servants took on new names, the Ohanzee and the Senka, to represent their new occupation and swore to protect the two new countries from the shadows as diligently as they had done Renatus.

Six hundred years passed, gradually changing the seasons, landscapes, and even the hearts of men—slowly fading the fragile bonds between friends, families, and kingdoms. In Marise, the people strove to rediscover the knowledge lost in the Fall, to conquer the world around them, and to unlock its vast mysteries. In Chiyo, however, the people clung steadfast to Gared's ideals, seeking to understand nature's complexities, harvesting its bounty, and striving to live in harmony with the lands around them.

Both countries flourished, learning and progressing, and growing more dissimilar with each passing year. Eventually, blood ties between Chiyo and Marise faded, and the blissful unity of the two nations lessened to little more than diplomatic relations.

---

Caelan and Alala trudged along the narrow dirt path through the trees. Their joints ached and their feet burned from a long day of walking. Today was yet another in a seemingly endless string of days spent moving furtively from one village to the next. Deep down, Caelan wondered if they would ever find a place where she felt safe enough to stay for more than a few hours. Did such a place even exist?

Still, a more pressing need was to reach the next village. Caelan desperately hoped they had not taken the wrong turn at the river. Twilight had set in, and the warm spring afternoon was quickly becoming a cold evening. The woods here at the foot of the mountains were so dense and the brush so overgrown that it was difficult to tell a footpath from a gap in the trees. She pulled the blanket tighter over her baby's chest, hating the idea that he may have to spend the spring night outdoors.

"I'm sure the village is not far ahead, M-M-...I mean,

Caelan," Alala assured her, sensing her companion's discomfort.

Caelan winced. She had given up her former name when she fled her home. "You would do best to forget you ever knew a woman by that name. It will bring us no good now."

"My apologies, it will take me some time to adjust," Alala mumbled, now avoiding Caelan's eyes by intently studying the path ahead. "Oh! We must be close. I think I just saw someone ahead!"

"Impossible, there would never be a village so deep in the woods..." Caelan's argument was cut short by a gasp. Several feet in front of them, three men stepped out from the trees, blocking the path.

"Bandits?" Alala asked, her voice wavering with fear.

"No, there are no bandits in Chiyo." Although her own voice was confident, Caelan felt uneasy. Crime in Chiyo was practically non-existent, but there was another reason why she knew that these men were not bandits. The long ponytails worn high on their heads, the swords at their hips, and their imposing stance immediately identified the men to Caelan as members of the Senka. There was no doubt that the same thoughts were going through Alala's mind too. After all, the Senka were a group both women knew *very* well.

*Why did they come searching for us? How could they have found us here?* Caelan's mind raced, and she felt her feet moving backward of their own accord. Running would be pointless.

There was no use in resisting now. She willed herself to stand firm, even when Alala gracelessly bumped into her as she too was carried backward by her rebellious feet.

"What are you doing here?" the first shadow questioned, moving smoothly and silently to close the gap between them with each word.

Caelan hesitated. Those were neither the words that she had expected to hear nor the accent she had been afraid to hear them in. The men were now close enough that she could distinguish the features of the one confronting her. She didn't recognize him, and it was clear that he did not recognize her either.

Realization and relief dawned on her simultaneously. These men were not from the Senka. They must be members of their counterparts, the Ohanzee. The wheels in Caelan's mind spun rapidly into motion. There *was* one place where the three of them would be completely safe. It was a place the Senka had never found no matter how hard they had tried— the hidden stronghold of the Ohanzee. This was a most fortuitous coincidence. If only she could get this situation to go her way.

"We are merely travelers, seeking shelter for the night," Caelan replied, choosing each word with care and unconsciously pulling the blanket even tighter over her sleeping son's chest.

"There are no villages for at least half a day's walk from here. What is your *real* reason?" The man's voice was filled with suspicion.

So they *had* taken a wrong turn at the river. It seemed fortune was on their side tonight. "Surely if you are here, then there must be a village nearby," she said shrewdly.

All three men remained silent, their stoic expressions unchanged. Caelan decided to try a more direct approach. "You are members of the Ohanzee, are you not?"

"Your voice is thick with the accent of Marise. What are your real intentions? Speak quickly, before I become impatient." The man's words were more like a growl than a command.

It was time for Caelan to play her hand. The very thing that had set Alala and her on their wandering path could also secure their future. She may yet be able to prevent a terrible event from happening and find a safe home at the same time.

"Two women and an infant alone in the forest are hardly a threat to the Ohanzee. As a matter of fact, I might even be able to help you. In return for a favor, of course. I want sanctuary—a home in your village—for the three of us."

Alala's eyes became as wide as saucers at Caelan's bold request.

The man looked truly beastly with his eyes narrowed and figure silhouetted in the fading light. "While I agree you do not appear to be a threat, I cannot imagine how two women and a child alone in the forest could possibly help us. Then again, no ordinary woman would even know of our existence. You will explain yourself, and afterward I'll consider your request."

Caelan drew in a deep breath. She could afford to omit no details for fear that they would not believe her. This may also be the only opportunity to preserve the peace between Marise and Chiyo. "I have learned through my husband that King Casimer plans an attack on Chiyo. He is sending five of the Senka to the Manor in Niamh to assassinate the Royal Family. They will be disguised as servants and are possibly employed in the Manor as we speak."

The man's face showed no reaction. "So, Casimer has finally abandoned the pretense of diplomacy." His voice was filled with scorn. "Why is your husband not here with you?"

"He is wholeheartedly devoted to the plan."

"And you are not of the same opinion?"

"I would not be here if I were. I am neither so arrogant nor so foolish as to look down on the way of life of an entire country. The man I married no longer exists as far as I am concerned, and as such, I have permanently separated myself and our son from him. I certainly have no intention of raising my child to follow such an example." Her voice flared with bitter passion at the last statement.

The first man seemed unmoved, but the white-haired man behind him spoke up. "This is not an allegation we can take lightly. We will grant the three of you shelter and food for the night. In return, you will elaborate fully on how you came to this knowledge as well as how you came to be here." His voice took on a warning tone. "But know this—if you speak the truth, we will grant your request. If you lie, your child will be the sole survivor."

TWENTY YEARS LATER

# 1

## THE HEIRESS OF CHIYO

*Nerissa*

"What harm could possibly come from reading a book?" Nerissa scoffed, eagerly running her fingers over the creviced cover of the aged tome in her hands. "None at all," she finished without waiting for her friend and fellow conspirator to answer. She turned the book to examine the binding with greedy fascination.

"You say the same thing every week when I bring new books. And don't get attached to that one. I told you it isn't staying! It's not like you don't have enough books to read already." Charis pointed to the other volumes she had brought. "I don't think all of these will fit in the usual hiding place. Where are you going to put them?"

The question successfully snapped Nerissa out of her rapture. She paused for a second, eyeing the stack with one eyebrow raised and her lips twitched to one side in thought. "The only ones my parents will have a problem with are the scientific texts that were written in Marise. This mathematics book is a little thick, but I think all four will still fit in the usual spot. You're right though," she said with a doleful sigh, "I ought to put them away before someone comes by."

Nerissa laid down the object of her fascination, pulled up the loose stone tile in the floor, and began nestling the four taboo books into their hidden nook. Charis seized the opportunity and scooped up the discarded volume, cradling it in her arms.

"I'm the Heiress of Chiyo, and yet I'm reduced to hiding books from my parents in a hole in the floor. Honestly, I don't see why I should have to go to such lengths," Nerissa complained. "Ugh, this one isn't going to fit!"

She removed the topmost book and began rearranging the others to make more room. Noticing Charis' silence and fearing she may have sounded ungrateful, Nerissa quickly continued, "I am ever indebted to you for smuggling these in for me week after week. Do my parents really think that we can ignore Marise's development forever? Even if we don't utilize their technology, we should try to understand how it works!"

When Charis still didn't reply, Nerissa looked up to find her halfway across the room with the antique book cradled in her arms. Her viridian eyes glinted with suspicion from between long locks of golden-brown hair as she slid the stone tile back into place and then hurried to her friend's side.

She peeked over Charis' shoulder and pointed at a nondescript flap on the ancient book's binding. It was hardly noticeable without close inspection, but few details ever escaped Nerissa's sharp eyes. "What is that for anyway?"

Charis faltered, "I-I don't know. I think I remember seeing a crystal inside when I was little."

15

"I hope it didn't break," Nerissa said, lifting the book from Charis' hands with an impish grin before scurrying away. She pulled aside the airy curtains surrounding her bed and flopped into a mountain of aqua and ivory pillows. "It's very odd to see a crystal embedded in a book. I've seen them in nearly everything else but never a book."

Charis settled in opposite her and leaned back against the curving lattice that spanned the two thick posts at the foot of the bed. "Maybe it was more common in the past. There are so few books this old that it would be hard to know for sure."

Nerissa's only response was a distracted hum and nod of agreement as she skimmed through the yellowed pages.

"Which reminds me...have you heard about all the crystals around town that have shattered?" Charis asked casually.

Nerissa's head snapped up from the book to meet her friend's hazel eyes. "Shattering? On their own? Are you sure?"

"That's what I've heard. I haven't seen it happen with my own eyes. Considering your interest in crystals, I thought you would have heard about it before me." Charis' brow furrowed. "I'm surprised by your reaction. You seem alarmed. I thought it was nothing more than some kind of strange coincidence."

Nerissa frowned. She wouldn't admit it, but she had long been envious of how openly people spoke with Charis. As the University President's daughter, Charis had connections all over the city. And while those people freely shared the latest gossip and rumors with her, they tended to be overly polite and formal in the presence of the Heiress.

"Do you know how many have shattered?" she asked.

"I don't know *exactly* how many, but more than a few

16

people have mentioned it to me."

"That's too bad," Nerissa said with a crestfallen sigh.

"Why does it matter how many? Is there actually some significance to the occurrence?"

"It used to be a common belief—or superstition, according to my Mother—that, if a crystal breaks suddenly, it is an omen that a significant change is coming. It doesn't indicate whether it will be something bad or good, just a sudden change. The theory is that the natural flow of energy through the crystals changes so rapidly..."

Nerissa cut short her technical explanation upon noticing that Charis' eyes had taken on a glazed look. "Well, never mind the details. I'll have to see if Tao has heard anything when I talk to her tonight." She patted the book in her lap. "You won't mind if I take this to show her, would you?"

"Of course I mind! It's a precious keepsake from my mother! I told you my father will get mad at me if he finds I took it out of the house. I brought that book so you could see it, not borrow it."

Nerissa summoned her best pouting face. "You don't even trust it to your oldest friend in the world? I'm hurt, Charis. Truly, I am."

"Don't you dare! You think you can manipulate your way into getting anything you want from me, but it isn't going to work this time. I know your tricks very well. After all, I'm *your* oldest friend in the world."

"Cha*ris*," Nerissa whined. "We said we'd do anything for each other!"

Charis sighed. "Not a chance. This is definitely *not* one of those things." She paused momentarily, and added, "And we were five when we promised that!"

"That is exactly my point! You are far too attached to the past. Think of letting me borrow this as the first step towards learning to let go," Nerissa said, nodding her head encouragingly.

For a second, it seemed that Charis' resolve might finally be weakening, but then she said, "Wait...you brought up that promise, not me! Nerissa, I'm serious. Father is just as protective of this book as I am. He would be angry if he knew I had even showed it to you!"

Nerissa had learned a long time ago that it was generally unwise to push Charis too far, and she knew she had reached the limit this time. She relinquished the book to Charis' anxious hands even though she desperately wanted to examine it further.

Despite her lighthearted exterior, Nerissa had other reasons for wanting to hold on to the ancient book longer. Based on her initial perusal, Charis' book was no more than a collection of lore. Still, any book *that* old was bound to be filled with all sorts of fascinating history. Moreover, there was something intriguing about it that she couldn't quite put her finger on. This was made more tantalizing by the fact that, for some mysterious reason, no one was supposed to actually read the book. What is a book for if not to be read? A thorough investigation was most certainly needed. Before she could ask to see it again, however, Charis had tucked it securely back in her bag.

Charis grumbled as she gathered last week's supply of books and stowed them in the bag as well. "I have to get home now. Amon returned from his most recent trip this afternoon, so I have to cook for three tonight. Amon's frequent trips home are obviously suspicious. I don't know how my father can be so blind to it."

"Oh, yes. Amon is *obviously* a horrible man," Nerissa teased. "He is handsome, well educated, dedicated to his studies of historical art, and he frequently travels home to visit his widowed mother. And let's not forget his most grievous trait of all—he shows a special interest in his mentor's daughter. Who in their right mind would do *that?* It's scandalous, really."

"You know that I have more reasons to distrust him than that! Not the least of which is the fact that he is King Casimer's nephew. Am I the only one who still remembers that Casimer once attempted an attack to take over Chiyo?"

Nerissa's eyes narrowed, but that didn't stop Charis from continuing. "That alone is reason enough to be suspicious— and don't start with your diplomacy lecture. Amon is up to something. I can sense it. His interest in me is a part of the act." She put special emphasis on the last statement.

"The attack was nearly twenty years ago, and diplomacy has been restored for the last fifteen," Nerissa said. "It is a thing of the past. Besides, you can't judge a person's character by their relatives."

Seeing her friend's visible exasperation, she added, "Fine. You're right, he is clearly a man of dubious intent."

"You and Father are far too trusting!" Charis said, but the vehemence of her protest was dulled by the visible twitch at the corner of her lips.

"And you are far too suspicious. Fortunately, as long as we have each other it will balance out," Nerissa said with a contagious grin.

Charis tucked an errant lock of coppery hair behind her ear. "I suppose so," she agreed before hefting the book bag onto her back with a soft groan. She looked over her shoulder as she walked out the door. "One day you're going to break my back with this bibliophilic addiction of yours!" Her parting words and laughter echoed through the hallway.

Nerissa closed the door and smiled to herself while she crossed the room to slide open the delicate paper-paneled doors that lined the far wall. A gentle breeze swept in, carrying with it the faint, familiar scent of bergamot and cedar. Air stirred the slender crystal chimes that hung between the doors, filling her ears with their soothing, musical tinkling.

Returning to the other side of the room, Nerissa seated herself at the dressing table and examined her reflection. The table was covered with a sparkling array of glass bottles and jars in every shape and size, simple and ornate, filled with creams and powders in every color of the rainbow. A long red cloth containing brushes of myriad number and variety was rolled into a neat, scroll-like bundle. On the right-hand side of the table, were three rows of short, fat bottles of sparkling nail lacquers, all identical except in color. Next to those stood a small stack of boxes containing false lashes, some plain and natural, some interwoven with decorative crystals. Jars with tiny glass beads in the bottom held dozens of hair combs and pins for easy viewing.

This was her one vanity, and she lacked the willpower to resist the newest powder or shadow color. In Nerissa's mind, her hair and cosmetics were the only things that really made her appear feminine. She supposed her face was pretty enough—with the proper makeup—but she had the extraordinary misfortune of inheriting her father's handsomeness rather than her mother's delicate facial features. It was her additional misfortune that she never developed much by way of feminine curves either. If it weren't for creatively designed corsets, she would have no bosom whatsoever.

After scrutinizing her appearance in the mirror, she piled her long locks on top of her head and deftly secured them with two sparkling hairpins. She spritzed two puffs of strawberry and rose perfume in the air above her head and silently thanked her mother for at least passing on such lovely hair. Then she grabbed a folder of notes and stepped into the hall.

If Nerissa's room could be described as breezy, the hallway was a tunnel of swirling wind. The red fabric banners fluttered away from the walls, such that the symbol of her country emblazoned upon them, the golden phoenix, seemed to be flying. She glanced into her parents' room, their studies, and the vast meeting room as she walked by, unconsciously obeying the irresistible instinct every person feels upon passing an open door. Nerissa was not at all surprised that every room in her family's private quarters was empty. With preparations well underway for the annual masquerade party the following night, everyone was busily at work elsewhere in the Manor.

When she pushed open the heavy wooden doors at the end of the hall, she was swept out from the isolation of the second floor into a hive of activity. The normally quiet great hall was abuzz with workers bustling from one place to another carrying decorations, setting up tables, and arranging flowers. Nerissa hurried down the sprawling staircase and scurried around the towering ladder one man was using to hang long strips of fabric from the ceiling. But despite moving through as discreetly as possible, her presence still attracted attention, and she was cornered several times by workers seeking her opinion. Though she wished otherwise, she could hardly ignore or divert their questions, so she answered each one as best she could.

Finally, at long last, Nerissa breathed a sigh of relief and strode through the open front gate of the Royal Manor. The peaceful country of Chiyo had no need for uniformed sentries standing watch at the gate, but Nerissa knew that there was a group of guardians who protected the Royal Manor itself in secret. She knew very little else about them, though on rare occasions she thought she had seen someone lurking in the shadows—places which had been vacant a moment earlier.

The first time she had asked her parents about them, her mother had said their very existence was a secret that should never be disclosed. As a result, Nerissa didn't know how many guards there were. She imagined that their numbers were likely few. There was only one time she knew of that anyone had dared threaten the rulers of Chiyo. And the guardians' success on that occasion was the very reason for the impending celebration.

Before she could go on to her ultimate destination, Nerissa had one stop to make at the boutique where both of her costumes for the following evening were being made. The shop was small, but the seamstress there was extremely talented and renowned for creating unique styles. Those qualities made her a favorite among all the nobles in Niamh, so it was natural that she be the one to design the costumes for most of the women attending tomorrow's masquerade ball.

This year was unusual because Nerissa had requested two costumes. She had asked for the second one be kept a secret under the pretense that she wished to surprise her parents. While Nerissa disliked being deceptive, the secrecy was vital to her plans for the evening. The second costume would give her the opportunity to mix with the other revelers as an equal.

The reason why she was so fond of the masquerade in the first place was because the masks and ornate clothing provided a sense of anonymity that could be achieved on one night each year. Yet, ever since Nerissa had become old enough to attend the royal ball at the Manor, she had lost even that one evening. Her mother had great fun dressing the whole Royal Family in matching or themed costumes, and she had no care for anonymity whatsoever. Although she didn't want to deny her mother that pleasure, it came with the unfortunate by-product of taking away the aspect of the masquerade Nerissa treasured most.

To be fair, it wasn't just the costume that made her identity known to all. One glance at the ring finger of her left hand was all it took. The golden phoenix, with its head and red enamel tail feathers facing to the right to represent the future, was worn by the Heir or Heiress of Chiyo. Her parents each wore similar rings, representing the past and present. Needless to say, she would *not* be wearing the ring with her second costume.

A tiny bell chimed as Nerissa pushed open the door to the dressmaker's shop. The front room served a dual purpose as both a showroom for the season's new designs and a fitting room, with curtained booths on one wall and mirrors lining the other. The dressmaker was nowhere in sight, so Nerissa entertained herself by idly examining a rack of blouses.

"Ahh! Heiress Nerissa, you must be here to check on your costume!" the woman said when she emerged from the back room. "Come and take a look! The last few days have been hectic, but the second one is nearly done."

Nerissa smiled politely and followed the woman into the backroom where bolts of cloth were neatly arrayed in a rainbow of color along the walls. There were several other dresses on mannequins around the room, but Nerissa's eyes were immediately drawn to one in particular. The dress was remarkable, with elegant ruching on the bodice and layer upon layer of fabric filling out the skirt. However, it was the color that truly set it apart—the crimson orange of sunset.

"I was a bit worried since this is the first time I've used this color dye, but I think it turned out rather well," the dressmaker said. She held up a long feather that had been dyed to match. "I'll be adding these to it tonight."

"It's beautiful," Nerissa breathed. "Do you need to check the fit once more?"

"No, I've been working on the embellishments and accessories, so I haven't made any alterations since the fitting earlier this week."

"Excellent, I look forward to seeing it finished."

"My husband can bring it to the Manor tomorrow afternoon," the woman said.

"There's no need for that. I'm sure you'll both be very busy delivering costumes to your other customers. I'll come by tomorrow afternoon myself. I don't want anyone to get a peek at the dress beforehand anyway." Nerissa winked as she returned to the front door of the shop.

"I couldn't possibly allow..."

"I insist," Nerissa interjected, cutting off the other woman's protests. "Besides, someone might wonder why I am having two dresses delivered and then that would ruin the surprise! As always, I thank you for your hard work."

"It is my pleasure, Heiress." The woman bowed as Nerissa exited the shop and stepped into the street.

The main avenue was filled with people. Rarely was it so crowded in town, but preparations for the following night's festivities were underway here as well. Booths and stands were being constructed in the grassy squares that separated the buildings on one side of the road from the other. Tomorrow night these streets would be overflowing with masked revelers. Unlike the elegant decorum of the masquerade at the Manor, the festivities in town were energetic and sometimes wild celebrations involving games, contests, food, and drink.

Although Nerissa had always lived in the Manor by the river, she felt particularly affectionate toward the heart of Niamh because it was where she had spent most of her youth. Even her earliest memories of the masquerade were of spending the evening on these very streets with Charis and her father, playing games and eating snacks until she felt sick.

Despite being the daughter of Chiyo's Blood and Bond, there had been no guarantee that Nerissa would one day inherit the rule of the country. Royal children were always treated the same as all other children in terms of schooling and discipline. That changed at age twelve when she, like others before her, began to learn about policies, procedures, and protocol from her parents and took on minor public responsibilities. During this time, her actions and behaviors had been evaluated by a secret council to determine if she was fit to receive the title of Heiress. She had no idea who the members of the selection council were. Nerissa had been approved of unanimously and was named Heiress on her seventeenth birthday. She had been the Heiress of Chiyo for three years, and now it seemed there were only a few citizens who still remembered her as the child she once was.

Nerissa was so lost in thought while she walked that she didn't even see the cream-filled pastry until after it was in her mouth. She blinked in surprise and then smiled broadly around the edges of the protruding confection. There may be few people in Niamh who remembered her as the child she once had been—but the stout, laughing man now standing in front of her was one of those few.

"So how is it? Do you think it is good enough for tomorrow night?" he questioned, leaning closer to her expectantly.

She swallowed the first bite and pulled the remainder of the pastry from her mouth. "Recruiting unsuspecting taste testers again, Pan?"

"Humph! You've been sneaking tastes of my cooking ever since you were this tall," he grinned, gesturing to the level of his knee with one hand. "It's about time the tables were turned!" His whole body shook as he chuckled so loudly that those passing by craned their necks to see what was going on.

Oh yes, Pan remembered the antics of Nerissa's childhood all too well. He was one of the most jovial people she knew, always quick to smile and laugh—and equally quick to bring about the same reaction in others. Nerissa had lost count of the number of times she blushed at jokes he had told in her presence. He had a habit of forgetting himself and saying off-color things occasionally.

A window above the bakery banged open, and Pan's wife leaned through. "Pan! You're not telling tasteless jokes again, are you?"

"Never, Addy, my dear!" he called back innocently. "How could you even think I would do that in front of such a refined lady?"

His wife tsked affectionately from the window. "If he makes you blush again, Nerissa, you have my permission to send him off to the farm for a few weeks until he learns to control his tongue!" Addy laughed and disappeared again.

Nerissa stepped into the shop, trailed closely by Pan. "I think that the pastry will be perfect for tomorrow night," she said with a smile. "Now that I have the taste in my mouth, I ought to bring a couple to have with our tea."

"Visiting with Tao today? I wondered what had brought you by," Pan said absently. He placed two confections into a small, waxed paper bag.

"Yes, since tomorrow night is the masquerade, I can't meet with her on our usual evening." Nerissa couldn't resist taking another bite of the sweet in her hand. "If I don't fit in my dress, I will hold you personally responsible, Pan," she said in her most scolding voice.

"My dear, you really shouldn't talk with your mouth full. I can't understand you."

Nerissa raised an eyebrow. She hadn't any food in her mouth at all when she said that. However, she did catch a glance of herself reflected in the glass case and realized she had a bit of cream on her cheek, which she quickly wiped away. "How much do I owe you?"

"For my favorite taste tester, no charge," Pan chortled, sliding the bag across the counter to her.

"The sign in the window says, 'No free samples.' You can't disobey your own sign, Pan."

"If you insist, today's fee will be a kiss right here."

No sooner had Pan pointed jovially at one of his rosy cheeks than a loud thump resounded from the ceiling, followed by an exasperated exclamation of "Pan!"

"She doesn't like it when I let others use her discount," Pan whispered conspiratorially.

Nerissa laughed and placed two coins on the counter. Then she dashed out the door, turning back long enough to stick her tongue out and wink. Pan simply put his hands on his hips and laughed.

To make up for the unexpected stop at the pastry shop, Nerissa cut through the gardens in the center of the city, which were just beginning to bloom. The wide legs of her pants rustled and stirred curls of fallen cherry blossoms with each step she took along the winding path. Throughout the gardens were tall stone sculptures, crafted to display the grand conquests and wondrous achievements of King Gared, the Hero of Renatus and one of Nerissa's distant ancestors.

In the center of the gardens, was the largest statue of them all. It depicted Gared atop a rearing horse, waving the flag of Renatus above his head in triumph. Nerissa was surprised to see a young man leaning casually against the horse's massive hind leg. His long black hair streamed behind him in the wind, and a sword hung at his side.

As she strained to get a better look, a lock of her hair was freed by an errant breeze and blew into her face. She quickly brushed it from her eyes, but, when she looked again, all that remained were long shadows stretching across the ground as a gust stirred still more soft pink petals from the trees. It all happened so quickly that Nerissa wondered if perhaps she had imagined the young man entirely, yet her senses tingled with an odd sense of foreboding.

# 2

## SHATTER

*Nerissa*

The feeling of foreboding lingered in Nerissa's mind as she arrived at the building that served not only as Tao's home, but also as her classroom and shop. Regardless of her age, Nerissa's mentor had seemingly boundless energy to channel into her "hobbies," which included teaching crystal classes to the town's children and running one of the largest crystal shops in Chiyo.

Tao's most intriguing work, and the reason why Nerissa met with her each week, was to delve deeper into the uses of crystals. She was always looking for new stones and new applications for them. Tao had a talent for combining gems— twinning, she called it—in unique and unprecedented ways so they could be utilized for highly specialized tasks.

In her younger days, Nerissa had been particularly vexed by one of Tao's first inventions: a combination of stones which can detect lies. It was a popular item among parents, judges, and merchants. These and other creations were sold in her shop along with individual crystals imported straight from Rhea, the distant mountain region of Chiyo.

Tiny crystals tinkled overhead as Nerissa entered the store, and an apprentice waved to her on his way into the stock room. Tao could be heard leading her students through the steps to identify a crystal's element: first by the shape and then by the color.

There was a little bit of time before the class ended, so Nerissa occupied herself by browsing the shop for new additions. One glass-enclosed case contained hundreds of fire-fire stones. Their sharp, jagged contours in sparkling yellows, oranges, and reds presented a stark contrast to the soft curves of the blue and purple water-water stones in the adjacent display.

On the opposite side of the shop, two women were exclaiming over the pure, clear spirit stones. They commented on both the remarkable quality and the inexpensive price. Spirit stones were the only crystals identified solely by color without regard to shape. Colorless gems of high clarity were very rare indeed—meaning spirit stones were prized above all others.

Wandering past the case of fire-air and air-metal stones, Nerissa paused to look at the most unique crystal in the collection. It was one of her personal favorites. The stone was a gradient of clear, blue, green, and pink with threads of silver within the stone itself; representing spirit, water, earth, fire, and metal, respectively. It was far more rare than even the clearest spirit stones, and as such, this particular specimen was not for sale.

A single stone that embodied all the elements was so astronomically rare that Nerissa would have doubted its existence if she couldn't see it with her own eyes. Stranger still, the stone didn't behave like any other. No matter what minerals Nerissa and Tao had tried to twin with it—and they had tried numerous combinations—it sat there as lifeless and unreactive as an ordinary rock.

The sound of rustling papers reached Nerissa's ears, so she tore her eyes away from the unusual stone and walked down the narrow hallway that led to the classroom. Holding the bag of pastries behind her back, she leaned against the door frame and waved discreetly to Tao.

The students, none any greater in height than Nerissa's waist, filed out of the room. Some paused and briefly bowed with formal greetings of, "Hello, Heiress Nerissa!" Others simply laughed and waved, calling out an informal, "Hello, Nerissa!" on their way past. Nerissa watched Tao carefully sort the papers on her desk, musing to herself about what the students would think if they could see how organized their teacher *really* was.

Her thoughts were brought to a sudden end by a crash from near the window, followed by a stifled curse from Tao. Before Nerissa could locate the source of the sound, Tao had already pulled a brush from its hook on the wall and began pushing tiny shards of a green crystal from the floor into a rubbish basket.

"Tao, that crystal! What..." Nerissa was cut off mid-sentence by a hiss from Tao.

"I'm such a clumsy old woman. It's a shame that I knocked over such a rare specimen," Tao said despite not having been anywhere near the window. "Earth-air crystals like that one can only be found in remote areas of Marise."

"Tao——," Nerissa began, but her protest was interrupted once again, this time by a pointed look from Tao along with a sharp nod of her head toward the other room. Her apprentice hovered near the door, doing a poor job of pretending to be busy dusting.

"Tao, that is a shame," Nerissa said, quickly amending her original statement.

"Indeed. Help me carry these upstairs so that I don't drop them too," Tao said dryly. She paused outside the door to bid goodnight to her apprentice, and Nerissa followed her to the second-story living area.

Located directly above the shop and classroom, Tao's personal quarters were as different from the first floor as night is to day. The area consisted of one large room that was both airy and spacious with a wide set of paneled glass doors opening onto a balcony. Bookshelves lined every available wall. They were stuffed to overflowing with volumes of literature and lore about crystals, their history, their myths, and their uses. Piles of papers and more books crowded the two tables in the center of the room. Some were closed with colored ribbons peeking out from the pages to mark important or interesting passages, and others were stacked atop one another while still open. There were even books protruding from beneath Tao's bed, apparently tucked away just before dreams overtook consciousness.

Tao started a fire in the small stove and put a gray kettle on top to boil water for tea. "So tell me, which lucky young nobleman will be escorting the Heiress to the masquerade tomorrow?" She asked the question without the slightest bit of shame in her voice.

Nerissa decided silence and a doleful look was the best answer. The idea of dating any of the noblemen of Chiyo was not particularly pleasurable. All of the young nobles she had the distinct displeasure of being acquainted with were less than discreet about their true intentions. After the third heartbreak caused by one of these self-centered leeches, Nerissa decided she would be much happier if she never married. Never mind that there were plenty of other men in Chiyo and that there were no requirements that she marry another noble. Her own mother had married a farmer, after all. Nerissa was thoroughly convinced that she would never find someone that was interested in *her* and not her station.

"You shouldn't choose to be alone because you had a few bad experiences, you know," Tao said.

*Oh, yes, I can*, Nerissa thought.

Tao crossed the room, opened a drawer, and pulled out a small cloth sachet. "Please humor an old woman and take this. It will help you find love."

"At this rate, I'll probably end up with some cocky nobleman. I'm much better off without love," Nerissa said, willing herself not to sulk in front of Tao. She withdrew the water-water crystal from inside the pouch and then shot Tao a questioning look.

"Water-water crystals attract true love. This stone arrived in today's shipment from Rhea, so I set it aside for you," she answered. "And you should be careful. If you keep saying that you'll end up with a cocky nobleman, it might happen."

Nerissa appreciated the gesture, even though she disagreed with Tao's sentiment. "It's beautiful. Thank you."

She had barely finished speaking when a muffled, musical tinkle drifted up from the first floor. A quick glance out the window confirmed that Tao's apprentice had finally left for the night.

An unreadable look flittered across Tao's face before she smiled faintly. "You were about to ask about the shattering crystals, yes?" She stood on her tip-toes, stretching to reach the top shelf of the tall wooden cabinet where she stored the tea leaves.

"So you've heard about them shattering too?" Nerissa waited for Tao to nod in confirmation before going on. "What is the need for secrecy? I've been told that crystals are shattering all over town, so it isn't like no one has witnessed it."

"Is that what your friend Charis says? She certainly has an uncanny ability to gather information. The phenomenon is causing a stir among many people because they believe in the omen that a spontaneously shattering crystal represents."

Nerissa knew omens could portend good or bad events, so she wasn't sure why Tao's statement left her with a heavy feeling in her stomach. "I can't help but wonder why so *many* are breaking though."

"You are a particularly observant girl, Nerissa. Have you seen anything unusual over the last few days?"

Nerissa twitched involuntarily a second before the kettle began its shrill whistle. She hoped that Tao hadn't noticed, or if she had, that she would think she had been startled by the kettle. "I've been busy the last few days preparing for the masquerade on top of my usual duties and studies. This is actually the first day that I've had some free time this week."

A knowing look crossed Tao's face, but if it was due to Nerissa's evasion, she chose not to pursue it. She gestured to a book that was opened and earmarked at the corner. "I have read that immediately preceding a great event, the building energy becomes so intense that it can sometimes become a tangible manifestation to anyone perceptive enough to sense it. Those who have experienced it wrote that it seemed almost as if the future were overlapping with the present."

Nerissa frowned, pushing the image of the disappearing dark-haired man out of her mind. "I am hardly a prophet, Tao."

"Indeed, you are not. There are very few true ones in the world. I simply think you are remarkably perceptive—you have been since you were a child."

Tao poured the steaming water into two tea cups and added a measured spoonful of rose tea leaves to each. Then she carried them out to the balcony where she and Nerissa both settled into their usual spots at the table.

"What do you think the omen could mean?" Nerissa asked, watching as tiny brown tendrils spiraled down from the leaves to the depths of her cup.

"I've been looking into it, but I haven't found any similar instances to what is happening now. In all of the documented cases I've come across, the crystals shattering were of the same type, so it was possible to get an idea of what sort of change was coming based on that. Now is different though. It is completely unprecedented as far as I can tell. All types of crystals are breaking, and the frequency is increasing every day." Her brow creased as she stirred her tea.

"Perhaps we are being pessimistic and the omen means

something good is coming," Nerissa suggested, trying to lighten the mood to squelch her growing unease.

"Perhaps. There is no use worrying about the future anyway. It's not like we can change it."

Nerissa nodded vaguely. She took a sip of the steaming liquid, closed her eyes, and willed the warmth to clear her mind.

"Speaking of change, I have a new invention!" Tao stood, excitement lighting her eyes.

Nerissa smiled over the rim of her cup. Tao was always keen to debut a new invention. "Well, let's see it!"

"Seeing it isn't the important part—this one is all about hearing!" The muffled words trailed back to Nerissa's ears from inside the house where Tao dug through one of her many piles.

Peering through the open doorway, all Nerissa could see of her mentor was the top of her peach-haired head. She turned back to watch the pink petals drift down from the branch of the cherry tree that arched over the balcony. It really was a wonder that Tao could find anything in such chaos.

An unfamiliar masculine voice called out from the doorway. "I haven't told anyone else about this yet! I was saving it to show you first." Nerissa's head whirled around, and there stood Tao with a mischievous grin on her face.

"What...did...you...say?" Nerissa spluttered, frantically blotting a spot of tea from her black pants. After turning so quickly, she had nearly sloshed the entire cup. Clearly, she must have misheard Tao's voice somehow.

"It is a combination that alters your voice." The deep

voice *had* come from Tao! Even her laughter was a deep, throaty chuckle instead of light and musical as usual. She pointed to the necklace embedded with crystals that snuggly encircled her neck. "There is one to lower your voice and one to raise it. I expect these may become quite popular—especially for the masquerades." Tao handed a second necklace to Nerissa, who quickly fastened it around her throat.

"How do they work?" Nerissa giggled upon hearing her own voice, now ridiculously high pitched—at least two full octaves higher than normal.

"When you talk, your throat vibrates. That is a type of energy of movement. The crystals in this necklace absorb that energy and transform it. Either a higher or lower sound is created depending on the combination of gems used. It's quite simple, actually."

"Simple, but brilliant," Nerissa squeaked and then giggled at herself again. "Do you have any more for tomorrow?"

Tao unfastened the necklace and laid it on the table. "No, I've only made these two prototypes so far," she answered in her normal voice.

"That's too bad. So tell me how you came about this discovery."

And so the two companions continued chatting and watching cherry blossoms drift away until the sun finally settled below the horizon.

---

Nerissa waved one final time to Tao, and an oddly nostalgic feeling washed over her before she turned back onto the path through the statue-filled gardens. It almost felt like this would be the last time she saw her mentor. That was a silly thing to think, of course, but she clutched the small glow lamp tightly in her hand and kept her eyes focused on the path ahead anyway. Hopefully, the tiny light would somehow prevent any other strange visions from reaching her eyes.

As she neared her family's estate, she was comforted by the familiar creaking of the large fans in the river. The fans had been built many years ago to provide relief from the sweltering summer heat in Niamh. Propellers deep in the water, turned by the flow of the river, kept the blades moving day and night, creating the constant breezes her home city was so well known for.

Although there were no more strange incidents on her way home, Nerissa's grip on the lamp did not loosen until she set it on the balcony adjoining her bedroom. When she collapsed into her pillows and the familiar scent of bergamot and cedar wrapped around her once again, there was only one thought on her mind. *Just what did the shattering crystals foreshadow?*

# 3

## AN URGENT MESSAGE

### *Shae and Desta*

Shae bolted upright in bed with a startled gasp. Sweat-ridden blonde locks clung to her face. A dream, no, a nightmare, had awakened her prematurely, long before the first glimmer of dawn. She pushed the damp strands of hair from her furrowed brow with shaking hands and took a few deep breaths.

Having collected herself somewhat, she reached into the wobbly night table next to the bed and pulled a pen and notebook from the top drawer. The pen was almost empty and the notebook cover was tattered and faded, the effects of frequent use. Shae's hand scribbled furiously across the page, trying desperately to record the entire nightmare in every essential detail so that nothing was forgotten. By the time she finished writing, her mind felt relieved of its burden but was also now completely awake.

After wrapping herself in a blanket to stave off the pre-dawn chill, Shae tip-toed through the small house, wincing at each creak from the cold floor. The last thing she wanted to do was awaken her daughter. While the tribulations of a heartbroken teenager were intense, they were of no comparison with what Shae had witnessed on the backs of her eyelids.

For most people, dreams were simply a fantasy. They were vivid in one's own mind yet had no direct impact on the waking world. For Shae, dreams were quite a different matter. She was a prophetess. It was a talent that had been passed for generations from nearly every mother to daughter in her family. So accurate were her visions of the future that her reputation was known throughout Renatus.

Shae's own version of the talent was particularly unique. Her visions came not only in dreams but in waking times as well. It was simultaneously a wondrous gift and a burdensome curse. The benefits were obvious. When her insight helped avoid an accident or revealed the solution to a difficult problem, it was incredibly gratifying. However, the negative side of seeing the future was often overlooked. The feeling of helplessness that she experienced upon witnessing a tragedy beforehand, like she had this night, was as terrible as experiencing the actual event. Even worse was the doubt, the questioning of skill, and the blame that occurred when a calamity went unpredicted. How could she foresee trivial events like her neighbor bringing over an extra pie but fail to see a warning of the tragic accident that stole away one of her most beloveds? She was now sure that the explanation of how her gift worked was as elusive as how it even existed in the first place.

Shae poured a cup of water from the brass pitcher on the counter and sank heavily into one of the wooden chairs. The moon had already set. Not a ray of light penetrated the windows, yet she did not bother to unshutter any of the glow lamps hanging about the room. Darkness' black fingers wrapped tightly around the familiar objects in the room, turning them into indiscernible shadows. The sound of the dried strands of the woven chair back crackling under her weight was her sole companion.

At times like this, silence was as deafening as a drum beat. It had been a very long time since Shae had felt so woefully powerless. The last time she had found herself in this position was after the untimely death of her husband. Though she had gradually come to terms with her grief and self-doubt, she was not going to let anyone else experience that pain if it could be prevented.

She sat for several minutes with her face in her hands, willing herself to think calmly. Her dream had foretold a catastrophe that would befall Chiyo. One that she knew would occur imminently. Though Shae had never been to the capital city, she knew the building she had seen engulfed in flames was the Royal Manor in Niamh. Above the burning Manor, a silvery-blue dragon rained balls of fire onto the building, shaking its walls from their foundation.

The imagery had been so intense that she felt the heat of the flames on her skin, and the horrified screams of fleeing costumed men and women echoed in her ears as if she had been there herself. A great phoenix had then risen from the rubble, crying in pain as it flew toward the western mountains and disappeared into the heavens.

The eeriest thing of all happened just before she awakened. The dragon somehow became aware of Shae's presence and swooped toward her with its fiery, gaping maw, chasing her from the dreaming world to reality.

As visions go, the interpretation of this one could not have been more straightforward. The dragon and the phoenix were the symbols of Marise and Chiyo. Two decades ago, King Casimer of Marise had attempted to assassinate the Royal Family of Chiyo and failed. The anniversary of the event was marked in the capital each year by a city-wide masquerade party.

Clearly, this dream was a warning that—tomorrow—on the night of the masquerade, King Casimer would make an attempt on the lives of the Royal Family again. Shae's heart ached at the memory of the phoenix flying toward the heavens. It could only bode the departure of the rulers of Chiyo. If events continued on their current course, this time Casimer was going to succeed.

Never once had Shae's visions been wrong, although they had been misinterpreted on infrequent occasions. Still, she had a hard time accepting this one would happen. She could not fathom that the tranquility their land enjoyed now could ever be destroyed. Even Casimer's initial attempt to assassinate the Royal Family had now faded to nothing more than a trivial bit of history.

The last part of the dream was puzzling. What could it possibly mean that the dragon had turned to her at the end? She'd never been anything other than an outside observer in her dreams. Was it a warning? If it were, Shae couldn't figure out the significance.

Knowing now that Casimer was planning a second attack, it was painfully logical that he would choose to strike at this time. The masquerade itself was an open mockery of his failure. The crowd of people moving freely into and out of the Manor would make an undetected entry easy. It was a bitter irony that in celebrating their previous success, the Blood and the Bond had become more susceptible to a second attack. Shae knew from experience that the likelihood of changing the outcome of this vision was small, but she was unwilling to accept such a fate without a fight. There was one option she could think of and even that had a small chance of having any effect whatsoever on the future.

She crept back to the bedroom to fetch her notebook, changed out of her bedclothes, and resumed her seat at the table. The glow of an unshuttered lamp illuminated her determined face as she copied every detail from her notes onto a blank sheet of her personal letterhead. Once finished, she folded the warning letter and placed it into an envelope with shaking hands. After dripping yellow wax onto the flap, she impressed her family's triangular seal into it.

The capital city of Niamh was a two-day ride from Shae's tiny farming village nestled at the border of Chiyo and Marise. She knew it would be almost impossible for a messenger to reach the city with the warning in time, but that was no reason not to try.

Shae pulled on her gray wool cloak and stepped into the cool gloam, making haste to the town messenger's home. She felt a twinge of guilt for knocking on his door at a time when even the birds had not begun to stir, but there was not a moment to spare in getting the message to Niamh. She hoped that she had not awakened his wife, Gladys, in the process. Gladys was the nosiest woman in the village, and in Shae's opinion, she was possibly the nosiest in Chiyo itself. This matter required the utmost discretion. If that woman found out, half the village would know of Shae's urgent message by sunrise and the rest would know by sundown. No doubt she had married Erik because his job made him the nexus of all news to and from the village.

A short time later, the door swung open silently, and a half-dressed Erik waved her into the house. To Shae's great relief, she could hear the sonorous snores of the busybody herself emanating from the adjacent room. With a smirk, Shae decided that the woman should be glad she didn't have the same fondness for gossip, or else Gladys' loud little secret would be known to the world. It was a wonder her poor husband could sleep with the walls practically rattling.

"Only something very urgent would bring you here so early, Shae," Erik said, rubbing the stubble on his chin as he lumbered stiffly toward the immense wooden table in the center of the kitchen. He picked up a kettle from next to the hearth and began filling it.

Shae pulled off her cloak, folding and refolding it anxiously in her arms. "It is. This message must get to Niamh before tomorrow evening."

Erik winced but it was unclear whether the reaction was in response to Shae's statement or the sound of a particularly loud snore from Gladys. "Tomorrow evening? Even if I leave now, it will still be nearly impossible to reach the city by then!"

"I know. This is a matter of the gravest importance and discretion. This warning must get to the Blood and the Bond before the masquerade tomorrow night. Even though it may already be too late, the lives of the rulers of our country are at stake." Her voice was filled with distress, despite being confined to a whisper.

Erik's jaw line tightened with every word Shae spoke, but he gave no further protests and asked no more questions. "I will leave immediately."

Shae placed the sealed note into his outstretched hand and departed. The echo of one last resonating snore rang in her ears as the door clicked shut behind her. On the other side of the door, Erik stared at the envelope. It would take too long to contact his cohorts. Delivering the letter directly to the Blood and the Bond was the sole option remaining. Minutes later, the lone witnesses to the horse and rider galloping from the town were the birds twittering at the first ray of dawn.

---

Desta's eyes fluttered open as the door to her bedroom creaked, and her mother quietly entered and sat down on the edge of the bed.

"Do you want some breakfast?" Shae asked. Her words were soft, but Desta could see there were dark circles under her eyes. Apparently, her mother had not slept well either.

"Not really." Desta's own voice was raspy and hoarse from crying herself to sleep the previous night. "Is something wrong?"

Shae gave her a wry smile. "Not really...at least, I've done all that I can about it now." She paused. "I do worry about a daughter who won't eat though. Depriving your stomach won't make your heart hurt less. I know that from experience."

"I'll keep that in mind." Desta was now absolutely sure there was something her mother wasn't telling her. Changing the subject was one of her favorite evasion tactics.

Shae was quiet for a moment, apparently lost in thought.

"I've learned something that will make you laugh." A mischievous glint appeared in her eyes as she spoke.

"What is it?"

"Gladys snores loud enough to shake the walls!"

"How did you ever find that out?" Desta pulled the blankets a bit higher so that only her head and the tips of her fingers were exposed to the cold morning air.

"I sent a message out early this morning with Erik. Gladys was still asleep while I was there." She chuckled a little, hoping to encourage the same response from her daughter.

Desta knew what her mother was trying to do, so she humored her with a forced laugh. "It's a good thing for her that you aren't nearly as big a blabbermouth as she is."

"You know, I thought the very same thing!" Shae said. She pushed an errant strand of dark hair away from Desta's face. "I have some work to do in the garden this morning, but if you want anything to eat, I'd be glad to make it for you."

"Thanks," Desta said noncommittally.

Shae stood and walked halfway to the door before turning back. "I'll make whatever you want."

"Don't worry. If I get hungry, I'll make something myself," Desta promised.

"Fair enough," Shae agreed.

The door was within inches of closing when Desta's overwrought mind finally processed the implications of what her mother had said. "Wait! You sent a message this morning?"

Shae hesitated briefly, not bothering to open the door further to answer. "Yes, it was nothing terribly important though."

"Oh, alright." *Like I believe that*, Desta added silently as the door clicked shut. If her mother sent a message away so early in the morning, it had to be related to a dream. No doubt Shae was keeping her own troubles to herself to avoid upsetting Desta further.

"Does she really think I'll fall for a lie that obvious?" Desta mumbled to herself as she dropped her socked feet over the edge of the bed.

It wasn't that she expected her mother to share every dream that she had. As a matter of fact, she kept the majority of her dreams to herself. There were many reasons to do so. For instance, some of the dreams revealed very private information about people's lives—things which were better left unsaid.

However, *this* dream had obviously shaken her mother. The circles under her eyes were visible proof of that. She would not have gone to Erik so early in the morning unless the matter were urgent. The situation piqued her curiosity, but that wasn't the main reason for her interest. Desta didn't have even a glimmer of the prophetic talent that ran in her family. Still, after years with her mother, she understood how much of a burden it could be. She wasn't about to let her bear this one alone.

Although she had not inherited her mother's talent, Desta seemed to have a different intangible quality working in her favor. For as long as she could remember, she had possessed uncanny luck. Regardless of how unlikely or unpredictable it was, somehow the most random and amazing things always managed to work out in her favor. She hadn't considered herself particularly lucky a few days ago when she stumbled across her—now—former boyfriend cuddling with a girl from the next village, but her mother insisted it was fortunate to know sooner rather than later.

She decided now was the time to put her luck to the test again. If her mother wouldn't tell her about the dream, then she would read about it for herself. There was really only a small risk of being caught in the first place since her mother would be occupied in the garden for quite some time prepping clippings for distillation.

Desta made her way to the kitchen where she made a point of rattling dishes loudly while going through the motions of making herself breakfast. The osmunda plants outside the kitchen window swayed back and forth as Shae sifted through them. Desta tapped on the window to get her attention and held up a bowl and spoon to show that she was about to eat. Shae wiped the sweat from her brow with the back of her wrist and smiled broadly.

With her mother's current whereabouts now confirmed, Desta decided the coast was clear to begin her reconnaissance. She dashed down the hallway to Shae's nightstand where the notebook was kept. Most people would call the small bureau rickety, Desta being chief among them, but her mother said that was part of its charm. Desta suspected her mother's affection toward it had less to do with "charm" and more to do with the fact that her father had made it. That did nothing to change the fact that it looked like it might spontaneously fall to pieces.

Desta hurriedly paged through the notebook to the latest

entry and began reading, her stomach tightening with each word. It was no wonder her mother was stressed. She had witnessed the assassination of the rulers of their country! Desta's own problems seemed inconsequential in that perspective. What was the loss of a boyfriend compared to the loss of lives? The message this morning must have been sent directly to the capital. She fervently hoped that Erik would reach Chiyo in time.

The front door suddenly slammed, and Desta hissed under her breath. She flung the book into the half-open drawer and thrust it closed with an audible rattle. Hoping nothing had broken, she leaped across the bed and reached the bookcase on the far wall seconds before Shae entered the room.

"There you are! What are you doing in here?"

"Looking for something to read," Desta replied with complete honesty.

"If you say so. I have an unexpected customer. Take whatever you like, and go back to your room, please." Shae's tone of voice indicated that this was not a welcome patron.

Desta grabbed several books at random from the shelves and scurried back to her room where she dropped them unceremoniously onto the small desk opposite her bed. Lately, she had been reading every book she could get her hands on, using the stories to temporarily escape from her heartbreak. Just a few days ago, her life had been peaceful and ignorantly happy. She expected a perfect future with her first love. And then, in one afternoon, her whole world had unraveled.

Desta's thoughts descended into despair, and she flopped into her desk chair, laying her head on her folded arms. Miserable thoughts lingered in her mind, and tears began to flow once more until sadness gave way to a dreamless sleep.

# 4

## THE CLEVER PROPHETESS

*Shae*

Though her name was known throughout all of Renatus, Queen Echidna's face was not, for she rarely made appearances outside of the royal court. Even Shae could never have foreseen that this dignified and regal woman would come to her tiny village, let alone her own home. And yet here the Queen was, sitting on her sofa.

Echidna's hands were folded languidly over one knee, displaying every perfectly lacquered nail. Silver rings embedded with polished stones adorned each finger. Somehow not a single hair was out of place in her glossy raven locks, which tumbled in a messy, but intentional, fashion out from beneath a green velvet hat. Looking at the Queen made Shae feel self-conscious of the dirt that was still caked beneath her own nails as a result of having her work in the garden suddenly interrupted. The Queen's hands obviously never performed such manual tasks.

Shae curled her fingers into her palms and willed herself

to stay calm and act deferentially. "To what occasion do I owe this honor?" she asked. *Besides my own continuing ill fortune*, she added silently. She was rapidly becoming aware that this visit must have been the meaning of the last part of her dream. It was good that Desta had returned to her room, and Shae sincerely hoped that she would stay there.

Echidna laughed lightly, elegantly covering her scarlet lips with the back of her hand. The stones in her rings glimmered and glossy nails flashed with her every movement. "That is what I am hoping you can tell me, Shae. You have no equal as a prophetess in all of Renatus, which is why I have come all this way to speak with you personally."

Shae tried to choose her words carefully. The sudden appearance of the Queen, in conjunction with the nightmare from this morning, had her on edge, but she didn't want to let it show. "I certainly never expected to host the Queen of Marise in my humble home. If you had sent for me, I would gladly have come to you, Your Highness."

Echidna's eyes narrowed, and for a fleeting moment her mask of pleasantness dropped. "I would prefer to keep my consultation with you in strictest confidence. For those in my position, discretion is of the utmost importance."

"I understand, Your Highness." Shae knew that discretion would be out the window in less than five minutes if Gladys spotted the dragon-marked carriage in front of the house.

"My husband gives no credit to 'nonsense' like prophecy. He would be quite angry if his name were associated with anything aside from the most respected and foremost scientific works," Echidna said. She waved a glittering hand in the air as if dismissing the words from her presence. "I, on the other hand, am of an entirely different opinion. I find the divination of fate to be an intriguing phenomenon. The information can be invaluable if it is obtained from a seer with genuine talent such as yourself."

"I am honored by your praise," Shae replied. She inclined her head slightly before continuing, feeling sickened by her own words. "However, I am afraid that you may have over-estimated my talents. I have had no visions about you, Your Highness."

Through the window, Shae could see the sun glinting off of one of the silver dragons emblazoned on the side of the Queen's carriage. Perhaps saying she hadn't had any visions about Echidna wasn't entirely true. The dragon in her dream had indeed come for her.

"There is no reason to be humble about your talents. My ladies-in-waiting tell me that you have the ability to see the future by gazing into crystals." Echidna waved her hands over the glass sphere that decorated the table like some vision of the future would appear in the glass by doing so.

Shae was taken aback by the sheer absurdity of the concept. That globe was a bauble her husband, a glass blower by trade, had made. Did Echidna truly think that a piece of artwork was a divination tool? Not only that, but this woman seemed to believe it was possible to summon visions at will. As part of the Marisianne nobility, Echidna was undoubtedly well educated. Yet it appeared that, in spite of all of the scientific knowledge she possessed, she had no understanding of the basic workings of nature.

Echidna was so caught up in her own thoughts that she failed to notice Shae's hesitation. "My husband plans an attack to take over Chiyo. His previous failure distressed him so greatly that I cannot stand the idea of it happening again. I want to know what can be done to assure him complete success." Her satiny voice gradually grew heated as she spoke, making it evident that she was no longer trying to hold back her excitement.

For her part, Shae was stunned to hear the woman speak so gleefully and so callously about plans that would lead to the deaths of many people. It was readily apparent that Echidna cared for no one beside herself and her husband.

Shae knelt down gracefully in front of the table on which the glass sphere rested and raised her hands up over it, mimicking Echidna's earlier movements. Staring into the depths of the orb as her hands brushed its sides, she pretended to scour the distorted forms within for hints about the future. Echidna's ignorance of the nature of Shae's talents provided an opportunity, and Shae seized it for all it was worth. She did something that she had never done before. Something that she had sworn to never do regarding her prophecies.

She lied.

"You are correct, Your Highness. I *can* divine the future through this crystal ball. I will tell you what I see for the King's plans," Shae said, trying to keep her voice steady. If deception could save even one life, then it was worth breaking her cardinal rule.

Echidna, meanwhile, had completely abandoned her aloof demeanor and inched forward to the edge of her cushion, perching there in rapt anticipation.

Shae's pulse raced, but she spoke slowly, pretending to be entranced by the pool of liquid colors in front of her. "I see a man with great ambition, focused and intent on success. He wishes to bring enlightenment to all in Marise and Chiyo. In doing so, he also plans to expand the influence of his power throughout all of Renatus."

"Yes, yes, I couldn't have described my husband better myself!" Echidna interjected with breathless excitement.

*I didn't need a crystal ball to see that,* Shae thought sarcastically. She continued on, aloud, adding an ominous tone to her voice. "This is not a favorable path. I see fire, bloodshed, and ruin. He was once defeated, marring his reputation with shame. A second attempt is also fated to fail and will ultimately bring disaster on himself. The attack will lead to the end of his rule and the loss of all he holds dear. There is no hope for success. He should abandon the plan immediately."

Echidna twitched visibly, her beautiful features now twisted into an enraged scowl. This was clearly not the answer she had expected to receive. She stood, towering over Shae as she raised herself to her full height, and kicked the small table onto its side with one dainty foot. "That is not possible." The words were uttered through clenched teeth.

Shae landed on one elbow after instinctively dodging the table and blinked up at the woman in surprise. The glass sphere rolled across the floor. For a moment, the warbling noise it made was the only sound in the room.

Shae stuttered as fear clenched her throat. "I-I-I'm sorry. I can do nothing more than tell you what I see." Could Echidna know that she had lied?

Echidna smoothed the front of her green velvet skirt with both hands and exhaled audibly. By the time she finally looked down at Shae, her composure had returned, but her eyes held a menacing gleam. "I should not blame you, Shae. You are simply a messenger who has no influence on the future. You can do no more than relay what you see in your visions."

Shae could barely contain her relief, but the feeling didn't last for long. Echidna turned her head, scanning the room. "Seers have both waking *and* dreaming visions, don't you? So you must keep a written record of your dreams. Perhaps you have inadvertently overlooked an insight from your sleep."

The color drained from Shae's face. If Echidna saw the notebook and found the entry from this morning, both she and Desta would be in grave danger. "I'm afraid I do not keep a written log of my dreams. They are as vivid to me as memories of my own waking experiences, so I have no need," Shae replied. A bead of sweat trickled down her back.

"I assume you will not mind if we take a look around." Echidna's predatory expression chilled Shae to the bone. Without waiting for a response, the Queen strode to the door and motioned to two men with long black hair who had been waiting near the carriage. She spoke with them quietly in the doorway. Shae strained to overhear but could not make out Echidna's words.

The pair of men bowed deeply to the Queen and strode into the house. One brushed right past Shae without acknowledging her presence. They searched the front room from top to bottom. Every drawer was opened and sifted through, and every bookcase and cabinet was scoured. They didn't bother to put any of the contents back into place.

"There's nothing here, my Queen," one of them announced several minutes later. Shae remained frozen in the middle of the scattered mess that was once her living room.

Echidna tapped a long nail against her red lips thoughtfully. "If the visions come in dreams, then it would make more sense for the notebook to be in her bedroom. Look there next."

The men nodded and headed to the hall. As the taller of the two placed his hand on the knob of the door leading to Desta's room, Shae spoke up. "That is my daughter's room. Please let me enter first so that she won't be startled."

Two pairs of brown eyes turned to Echidna questioningly. She responded with another flippant gesture of her hand, and the two stepped back to make way for Shae.

Shae's attempt to spare Desta from being surprised was futile, as the sound of the door opening jolted her awake. Her head jerked upward, and her elbow connected with a glass of water nearby, knocking it over. Its contents rapidly spread across the desk to the stack of books she had brought in earlier and began to seep into the one on the bottom.

Echidna's cronies ushered Desta away from the desk without giving her a chance to clean up the mess. Shae pulled her daughter over to where she stood near the window and wrapped her arms protectively around her.

"I'll explain everything later. Just don't say anything for now, alright?" Shae whispered furiously in Desta's ear. Desta gave no response but stayed quiet while her room was turned into shambles.

Their search of Desta's room turned out to be as fruitless as it had been for the front room. Shae followed along as they moved on to her own room, her feet heavy with dread. She hovered in the doorway, still holding her daughter tightly. There wasn't any point in running away since there was no chance of escaping from Echidna and her men.

When the taller of the two men opened the top drawer of the night table, tears sprang to her eyes. Every muscle in her body tensed in anticipation of the inevitable, and Shae desperately tried to think of a way to get them to spare Desta. And then, to her great surprise, the man closed the top drawer and moved on to the bottom.

Shae stared, stunned. Surely, he must have seen her notebook and pen!

But apparently he had not. He closed the bottom drawer and turned empty-handed to join his cohort in searching the bookshelf. They pulled each book off the shelf and thumbed through before tossing them into a growing pile on the ground. Shae was still in shock when he turned to Echidna and shook his head.

"There's nothing here, my Queen," he said.

"Very well, prepare the carriage to depart," Echidna commanded, unaware that anything was amiss.

She turned to Shae. "It seems you speak the truth. I will be on my way now. I expect that you will continue your normal routine like I had never been here. You will never speak of this visit again. Your neighbors have already been informed of my command and the consequences of disobeying me. They all have agreed that no one has come to visit this village in weeks. I suggest that you maintain that story as well. I will know otherwise."

"It will be kept in the strictest confidence," Shae replied

automatically, her voice wavering. Desta simply squeaked softly under Echidna's piercing gaze.

Echidna nodded in satisfaction then stalked out the front door, rattling the walls as it slammed closed behind her. Shae's knees buckled, and the world went black.

***

Shae opened her eyes and stared at the wooden rafters in the ceiling above her bed. A glance out the window told her that the sun had dropped below the horizon. Despite this, the room was bathed in the warm yellow glow of candlelight. She sat up and found Desta on a chair nearby with her knees tucked under her chin, her gaze transfixed on the window.

"Desta? Are you alright?" Shae asked.

Desta gave no response, so Shae stood, her legs riddled with the remnants of the wobbliness that she had felt earlier. "Desta," she repeated, kneeling down in front of her daughter.

"I was afraid to wake you, but I was also afraid that you *wouldn't* wake up," Desta said. Tears streamed down her cheeks, and she never released her focus on the window. "Once it got dark, I was afraid to unshutter the glow lamps because someone might be watching us from outside. I was too scared to sit here in the dark though."

Shae threw her arms around her daughter and stroked her hair. "There's nothing to worry about now. I am sure they are gone. We'll be fine as long as we obey her command to keep her visit a secret." She forced herself to sound upbeat. Shae would do anything she had to do in order to comfort her daughter right now. Getting back to a semblance of normality might help. "Why don't you return to your room and lay down while I make some dinner. You haven't had anything to eat since breakfast, have you?"

"I guess it is past dinner time," Desta replied, her eyes watery and wide.

Shae put her hands on the girl's shoulders and guided Desta to her room. After tucking her into bed, Shae returned to her own room and snapped the curtains shut. She did the same for each window she passed on her way to the kitchen. Still, she felt an eerie prickling sensation on the back of her neck as if she were being watched. It was truly fortunate that she had already sent the message to Niamh since there would have been no opportunity to do so now. She silently wished Erik a speedy journey as she prepared a pot of oatmeal.

The curtains had already been closed in Desta's room by the time Shae returned carrying a tray with a bottle of maple syrup and two bowls of oatmeal. It wasn't a typical dinner dish, but it would be easy on the stomach. She was surprised to see that Desta had not remained in bed. Instead she was at her desk dabbing at the book that had become waterlogged from the spill earlier in the day.

Shae's stomach sank when she saw exactly which book it was. That book was a precious heirloom, handed down through her mother's family for generations. Even though the leather cover was tattered and worn and bits had flaked away, Shae had always taken care to ensure that the crystal embedded in the spine had somehow remained in place.

She waited numbly while Desta removed the crystal from its hollow in the binding and carefully dried it as well. With a dismayed groan, Desta opened the cover to reveal that the water had soaked the first few interior pages as well. No matter how careful she was, the sodden fabric lining the inside cover peeled away more and more with every touch.

"You have some explaining to do," Shae said. "I assume you were actually snooping in my room when I found you in there earlier. I am extremely grateful that Echidna and her men couldn't find my notebook, but why *wasn't* it in the drawer?"

Desta swallowed and bit her lip nervously, clearly uncertain how to answer without getting into trouble. "Things really can't get much worse at this point anyway, so I may as well tell the truth," she said, hanging her head. "I could tell you were upset this morning. Since you had sent a message so early, I figured it must have been a dream that had troubled you. I went into your room to read your notebook while you were outside.

"I didn't hear you come in until the last minute, so I hurriedly tossed the notebook into the drawer right when you opened the door. I noticed it made a strange, rattling noise. I thought maybe the nightstand had finally broken, but it looked fine. I don't know what could have happened to your notebook after that. It should have been in the drawer."

"I'll be right back," Shae said before going to her bedroom and searching the drawers herself.

The top drawer was completely empty, and there was now a gap between the back and the bottom of the drawer. On a hunch, Shae lifted up the night table itself, and the notebook and pen slid out from the empty space behind the drawers. The rattle Desta had heard must have been the book slipping through the gap and falling to the floor. What were the chances of that happening? She returned to Desta's room with the notebook in hand.

"I can't believe you would sneak into my room and read my notes! But I suppose that today it saved us both from a great deal of trouble." Shae stopped her lecture prematurely as she realized Desta was not paying attention.

"Mother, you need to see this." Desta's voice was filled with amazement.

"Don't tell me if it's ruined. I don't want to know," Shae said, but she crossed the room to the desk anyway.

"Just look," Desta insisted.

Shae peered over Desta's shoulder, bracing herself for smeared ink and torn paper. Instead, she was drawn in by the hidden words which had now been revealed. She read them out loud. "In the time of King Gared, the seer Argia had a vision. Her vision was recorded and hidden within the covers of six books, where it will remain concealed until the time when it is meant to be read. When that time arrives, the cover of this book will become soaked with water, and these writings will be revealed." Shae glanced up and shared an astonished look with Desta.

Shae continued to read, her voice filled with awe. "The first part of the vision is as follows: One day Renatus will be divided into two nations, each equal, but opposite. In the days of this new world, the Destroyer of Peace will assume power. His ambition is to guide the future of the entire land. That fate belongs not to him, but instead to the One that will finish the work that King Gared started.

"The Destroyer is a creator by nature, and he fosters prosperity with his skill and vision. His ambition grows to consume him and blinds him to the betrayal perpetrated by those he trusts most. The Destroyer will slay the Peaceful

Ruler and claim her throne. In doing so, he will set the events in motion that will ultimately result in both kingdoms becoming nothing more than a memory.

"The Destroyer will fulfill his wish to rule Renatus, and even the memory of the Peaceful Ruler will be erased. But there is still One who can alter the course of the future. That person, the One who is no more, the One who has become another, the One who was seen before, the Reflection, will appear from the shadows."

Shae skimmed the remaining note. It went on to say that the crystal embedded in the binding would identify the One described in the prophecy by glowing when they held it. Below that were diagrams for some sort of machine. The accompanying text explained that the diagrams had also been divided into six parts and that the machine would be able to decode books that had been stored inside the accompanying crystals.

Shae couldn't fathom how a book would fit *inside* a crystal, let alone multiple books. Then again, if the note really dated from the time of the legendary King Gared, she supposed anything was possible.

"This is unbelievable," Desta said. "How could they have known back then that I would spill a glass of water on this book?"

Shae didn't respond right away. There was almost too much information to take in, and her thoughts were focused on other parts of the prophecy. She finally said, "The Destroyer of Peace described here must be King Casimer. This prophecy and my dream both warn that he will attack the Royal Family."

"Does this mean that Erik won't be able to deliver your message in time?" Desta asked.

"Even if Erik isn't able to deliver the warning in time, it seems there may be someone who can stop Casimer, after all," Shae answered. "We need to find the next book and figure out who it is that this prophecy describes."

# 5

## LATE AGAIN

*Nerissa*

The tolling of the morning bell and the gentle, constant creaking of the fans in the river were the first sounds Nerissa heard when she woke on the morning of the masquerade. For a few moments, she blinked out at the world with bleary eyes that were loath to take in the brilliant sunlight that filtered through the gauzy curtains covering the windows. A disquieting sensation tugged vaguely at the back of her mind like a storm cloud barely viewable on the horizon. It was a nervous feeling though not the sort of nervousness that came with excitement or anticipation. She couldn't quite put her finger on it, but it was like a feeling of...apprehension.

Tugging the blankets over her chin, she wriggled further beneath them and tried to figure out the cause. After some consideration—and nearly falling back to sleep—nothing came to mind. Truthfully, few things did this early in the morning. Perhaps it was a lingering worry from her conversation with Tao the previous evening about the shattering crystals.

Nerissa thought back, but she couldn't recall any of her dreams from that night. One of them must have been a nightmare that had faded to the edges of her memory. That seemed the most logical explanation.

Heaving a sigh of resignation, she mustered her resolve and threw back the covers. There was little use in dwelling on a bad dream, especially when there were far too many things to do and far too little time to do them. She couldn't linger in bed any longer regardless of how much she would have liked to do so. Bare toes contacted the cold stone floor as she reluctantly slid from the mattress, causing her to hop hastily from one foot to the other while lazily rubbing her eyes.

The drowsy daily ritual was interrupted by an odd crunching sensation underfoot. An uneasy knot formed in her stomach. Nerissa knew what she was stepping on before she looked down. Powdered bits, too fine to even be called shards, clung to her toes and the ball of her foot. The storm cloud in the back of her mind rumbled ominously.

She looked at her nightstand and was dismayed to find that both the lumpy light-blue water-water crystal and the pillar-like fire-metal crystal that normally sat there had shattered. Portions of their remnants were still on the stand, and the remainder had blown off onto the floor. There was no visibly apparent reason for them to have broken. Even if Nerissa had knocked them off the table in her sleep, the fall to the floor would have cracked or split them at most. A fall wouldn't reduce either stone to the piles of glimmering powder they now were.

Not wanting to call attention to the occurrence by summoning one of the maids, Nerissa glanced ruefully around the room for something suitable to use to clean up the mess. It was then that she saw the state of the other crystals. Or rather, she saw what used to be the other crystals.

She hissed an utterance under her breath not at all befitting an Heiress. Every one in sight had been reduced to powder at some point during the night. Nerissa stalked across the room, no longer caring about the cold floor, and snatched the silk pouch containing the crystal Tao had given her the night before. As soon as it was in her hands, she knew that there was no need to open it. There was no heavy lump inside the sachet. Even the newest gem in her collection had shattered. The knot in Nerissa's stomach exploded into a mass of quivering butterflies as the storm cloud rumbled once more.

She sank down onto the vanity chair, consumed with trying to puzzle out the meaning of this phenomenon. Facets in the red gemstone eye of the Phoenix flashed in the sunlight as Nerissa absently twisted her ring, too deep in thought to notice the sparkle. A moment later, her pondering was interrupted by a soft rapping.

Without waiting for a response from within, a woman peered around the edge of the bedroom door. "Good! You're already awake!"

Nerissa's mother, Rica, the Blood of Chiyo, was tall and slender like her daughter. Despite her age, not a single gray strand was present in the waves of golden-brown hair that were currently pulled into an elegant twist at the base of her neck. Merely the tiniest of crow's feet dared to mar her smooth complexion. Sky-blue gems matching her gown, cut and faceted into glittering teardrop shapes, glimmered from her ears.

Her mother was not only beautiful but also strong willed,

even tempered, wise, and fair. She was known to be resolute once a decision was made yet flexible when the situation required it. Rica glided across the room with a dignified stature that Nerissa hoped she would be able to match one day.

Nerissa shrank back into the tiny chair, drawing away from Rica's early morning exuberance like a shadow shrinking away from the light. It was bewildering how her mother could be so energetic at this time of day. Nerissa herself was more naturally suited to late night hours. It was another trait she had inherited from her father.

Rica floated across the room with the grace of a much younger woman, flinging open the windows and tying back the curtains. The edges of the curtains fluttered in the crisp morning air.

"Do you really have to do that," Nerissa groaned, covering her eyes as unfiltered light flooded into the room.

"Of course! You wouldn't be able to see your costume properly in the dark," Rica chirped. She clapped her hands together twice, and one of the handmaids scurried in from the hall carrying two garment bags. One was small, and the other was so large that it draped across her outspread arms.

Rica took the larger bag and smiled brightly. "These just arrived! I was so excited that I couldn't wait to show you."

The maid set the smaller bag on the bed and hurried back to the door. She curtsied briefly and then departed. Nerissa supposed that everyone must be in a rush today. But did they have to start doing it so early in the morning?

Rica's eyes twinkled as she untied the fasteners on the large bag, and she unveiled the dress inside with a flourish. The body of the gown was shining white silk. A stylized, stencil-like phoenix was embroidered with black thread so that it wrapped around the dress in a spiral from the skirt to the bodice. It really was beautiful. It must have taken the dressmaker and her seamstresses weeks of labor to complete. Nerissa felt a small pang of guilt for not sharing her mother's excitement.

"It's a lovely dress, Mother," Nerissa began. She chose her words carefully as she watched her mother's smile widened. "But isn't this supposed to be a costume?"

"Of course it is!" Rica laughed. "The matching mask is in here." She reached into the smaller bag, peeling away layers of tissue before handing the mask to Nerissa.

The mask was half-black, half-white with intricate gold embellishments framing the upper portion. Long black and white ribbons intermixed with strands of gold beads on each side. Nerissa turned it over in her hands and was greatly relieved to see that the mask, at least, did not have a phoenix tattooed on its face.

"Are your dress and mask the same?" she asked, already knowing the answer.

"Of course not." Rica's brow furrowed the way it always did when she thought Nerissa was acting silly. "The phoenix on mine is different. They match our rings."

"I see. Distinctly different," Nerissa mumbled without looking up from the mask.

"I thought the design was quite clever," Rica replied. Nerissa's lack of enthusiasm had no effect on her merriment. She took the dress from the bed and strode across the room to hang it in the wardrobe.

"So they have all shattered in here too," Rica said after closing the wardrobe doors.

"What do you mean?" Nerissa asked.

"The Principle Housekeeper reported this morning that every one of the decorative crystals in the Manor had shattered sometime overnight. She could see no apparent cause. No one within the Manor would have done such a thing, and there's no way anyone from the outside could have gotten in here undetected. I have to admit it's a mysterious phenomenon." Rica paused thoughtfully, her face unreadable. "Her primary concern was that my jewelry may also have been affected, but it was not."

Nerissa's brows knitted together. She turned and opened the vanity drawer that held her small, personal collection of jewelry. Unlike her mother, Nerissa preferred that her gems be left rough, uncut, and unfaceted to display their natural beauty. Not a single piece in the drawer remained intact.

"At least we seem to have found a common thread," Rica said, peering over her shoulder.

Nerissa's eyes met those of her mother. "The ones that have been cut and shaped haven't been affected."

Rica's face was again unreadable. "You should stop by and share this information with Tao. Perhaps she can offer some insight."

Nerissa frowned. Tao's area of expertise was a bit of a sore subject between Nerissa and her mother. Neither of her parents held the study of crystals and their usage in high regard. Rica considered it barely a step above astrology or telling fortunes with cards. Even Tao's most useful inventions only worked for some people. That inconsistency was the main factor influencing why Rica disregarded their study. The other contributor was that her mother was one of those for whom crystals did not work. Nerissa sympathized. It was difficult to believe in something that you couldn't replicate with your own hands, but that was no reason to disregard the use of them entirely. Requesting Tao's insight in this circumstance was indicative of the level of her mother's concern.

"I doubt I'll be able to before tomorrow," Nerissa replied.

"That will be fine as well, I'm sure..." Rica's voice trailed off as a soft breeze washed through the room, carrying with it a musical tinkling from the direction of the balcony doors. Above the doors hung Nerissa's precious spirit chimes, still swaying and sparkling merrily in the gentle current of air. They were completely whole. "Well, *those* are obviously not as fragile as they appear."

"Few things are exactly what they appear to be," Nerissa said. Rica's comment had referred to her objection to purchasing the chimes in the first place. When Nerissa had been much younger, she had begged her parents to buy them for her. Rica had initially refused to do so because of their delicate appearance. Spirit crystals were rare, and their price reflected that rarity.

The seven slender points dangled from wires as fine as hair. It looked like even the most gentle breeze could damage them. Nerissa's father had convinced Rica to change her mind, upon Nerissa's promise to take "extra-special" care of them. In truth, the stones were deceptively robust. Once, they had fallen from the ceiling, and Nerissa had thought they would be ruined. Yet they somehow survived the incident undamaged.

"It seems a masquerade surrounds us," Rica said with a wink. Her cheery mood was quickly returning. "Speaking of which, our masquerade party is just hours away, and you're not even dressed for the day! One day someone will see you in the morning and then everyone will find out that you're not always as energetic as you seem."

"Actually, I'm not feeling very well this morning." Nerissa's tongue felt heavy although the statement was at least half true. The revelation about the shattered crystals and the distant rumbling in the back of her mind had left her feeling decidedly unsettled. However, she knew that her mother would think that she was referring to her physical well-being. Nerissa disliked being deceptive, but this was a necessary step in order to pull off her plan tonight.

Reacting exactly as Nerissa had anticipated, Rica reached out and touched her daughter's forehead and cheeks tenderly with the back of one slender hand. "You don't feel overly warm," she said, still smiling despite her voice being filled with motherly concern. "Is it a headache and sour stomach?"

Nerissa nodded vaguely in response.

"It is probably allergies caused by all the blooms." Rica gave the diagnosis with a confident nod of her head. "Maybe you should cancel your training this morning."

"If it is allergies, moving around may help me feel better," Nerissa suggested. She felt her cheeks warming from shame. "Besides, I doubt that Einar would consider anything short of death as a viable excuse for missing a day of training."

Rica laughed knowingly as she walked to the door. "I think you're right. Einar is as stubborn as he is a good teacher." She paused in the doorway with one last request. "You do look a little flushed so be careful not to overexert yourself. It would be terrible if you were too sick to attend the masquerade. You wouldn't want to miss the festivities, and you have social obligations as well."

"Thank you, Mother. You're right. The last thing I want is to miss the party," Nerissa replied. That much was completely true. Rica nodded in understanding and closed the door behind her.

Nerissa crossed the room, approaching the crystal wind chimes that were dancing in the sun. She reached up to cup one of the transparent points in her hand, and hundreds of tiny rainbows danced across her skin. For a moment, she watched, awestruck by the simplistic beauty of the twirling stone.

Tao had said that you could often determine the changes coming based on the type of crystal that shatters. In this case, the spirit crystals were the only ones unaffected, so it seemed that whatever change was coming would affect all aspects of life except spirit. What could that possibly mean? It was perplexing. Still, as Tao had said, there was no sense worrying about what the future held. It would come to reveal its mysteries soon enough, and right now, there was not much time to dwell on those matters.

Out of the corner of her eye, Nerissa spotted movement in the practice fields beyond the gardens. Every morning began with some form of exercise. The practice was intended to improve coordination, mental agility, and stamina. A strong mind and a healthy body were qualities that were important for a ruler. After a furtive glance at the clock on her nightstand, she realized that she was about to be late for this morning's archery lesson.

Her instructor, Einar, was a strict teacher who demanded nothing less than perfection from his students. Even though Nerissa had a knack for the sport, this did not translate into her actually taking much pleasure in it. Quitting wasn't an option, however; so she simply went through the motions and used it as an exercise to help focus and clear her mind. As far as she was concerned, hitting the target was more the result of good concentration and discipline than physical prowess.

---

After a quick change out of her night clothes and a breakneck dash through the halls, she arrived at the practice fields. All she could do was hope that she wasn't late. As Nerissa tried to think of a good explanation in case she was tardy, a deep, masculine voice boomed just ahead of her. Nerissa groaned inwardly. Einar always greeted lateness the same way.

"An Heiress is to perform her duties, not make excuses about why she is late for them," Einar yelled.

*Late again*, Nerissa thought. She vowed to herself to wake earlier from now on, like she did every time this happened. Without waiting to be told, she began the usual punishment of running six laps from the first target to the garden walls.

This was definitely not how she wanted to start the day, but she had learned long ago that it was best not to try to argue with Einar. He was a tall, well-built man, and though not overly muscular, he was far from weak. Between his physique and his manner, he had a commanding presence that could intimidate even those twice his size.

"You could save yourself a great deal of running if you'd get here on time," Einar called out.

"It's not like I planned to be late," she huffed. It was as much of a defense as she could muster.

"It makes no difference to me. The results are the same no matter what your intentions were," he replied, shaking his head sadly when she passed on the second lap. The disappointment in his voice humbled Nerissa more than the scolding—it always did. She hoped that he would have nothing further to say by the third lap.

Fortune was not on her side.

"Your mother said you weren't feeling well. She asked me to go easy on you today, but you don't look sick to me," he commented, eyeing her suspiciously.

Nerissa wondered how her mother had managed to talk to Einar in the short span of time between leaving her room and Nerissa's arrival at the practice field. "Running seems to be helping," she muttered under her breath. She picked up her pace to escape his scrutinizing look. Lying was always so much harder than telling the truth. Nerissa had never been good at it, but it was especially difficult to get away with anything around Einar. That man seemed to know everything.

Midway through the fifth lap, Nerissa realized that she was hardly even winded. She really must have been serving this punishment often.

As she passed by again, Einar rolled his eyes up to the sky and lamented, "Why are my two best students both delinquents?"

Nerissa had lost count of the number of times he had said that to her. She had no answer, but she was secretly glad not to be his only delinquent student. She had often wondered who this other student was. Out of curiosity, she had once asked Einar. His response had been that he was not at liberty to share who his other students were. Matters of privacy he had said. If his other "delinquent" student were getting private lessons, then they were likely from one of the other noble families.

Nerissa mentally added archery lessons to her repertoire of conversation topics for the masquerade. It would at least break up the monotony of the usual polite conversations about the weather and similar small talk. Maybe she could figure out who Einar's other delinquent was.

Einar abandoned his post for the remaining lap to begin preparing the targets, leaving Nerissa to finish running in blissful silence. Afterward, she put on her practice clothes and chest protector and pulled a four-fingered glove onto her right hand. Her bow, nearly an inch taller than herself and made of curved bamboo, had also been used by her mother when she'd taken lessons from Einar.

At Einar's signal, Nerissa pulled an arrow from the quiver, nocked it, and raised her arms overhead. She slowly drew back the bowstring, simultaneously pushing the bow away with her left arm. She focused on both the familiar motions and the feeling of the arrow's fletching brushing behind her ear. Aiming the arrow at the target, she cleared her mind of all worries about shattering crystals or the many tasks to be done later. The sooner she shot these arrows perfectly, the sooner she could be done with practice. All that existed was the target, and she reached out to it with her mind, visualizing the arrow flying effortlessly through the air before striking the center. With the image firmly embedded in her mind's eye, her fingers released the string almost of their own accord.

Einar said nothing, which meant that the shot was good.

Praise from Einar was a rare occurrence indeed. He only gave it for truly outstanding shots, and he was a difficult man to impress. But Nerissa had not missed the hidden compliment in his earlier remark about being one of his two best students. While she nocked the next arrow, she idly wondered who was actually the better of the two. Whoever they were, it would be interesting to test her skills against them in a competition one day.

"Focus!" Einar barked from a few feet away.

Nerissa sighed, certain that the man really was able to read her mind. She forced herself to focus on the target ahead. The rest of the practice continued in much the same way, with Nerissa concentrating on form, step by step, and Einar watching for even the tiniest mistake or break in concentration.

Her shots early on were excellent, but by the end of practice she wasn't doing as well. It didn't make much of a difference to her at that point. She felt awake and refreshed, and her previous worries had been put out of her mind. Einar dismissed her with a clap on the back and a stern reminder not to be late next time.

Nerissa assured him that she would not and then hurried away from the archery range to look in on the final preparations in the gardens. The Manor and its surrounding gardens were separated from the acres of open grass by a tall stone wall containing only two doors. She detoured to the farthest end where the wall curved in and intersected with the exterior of the main house. Here, she crept through the rarely used door behind the greenhouse, which also happened to be located immediately below her bedroom.

The door creaked and groaned on hinges rusty from

disuse as she pushed her way through. Inside, a trellis covered with intertwined vines extended from the ground to the bottom of her bedroom balcony. When she was younger, it had served many times as an impromptu exit and entrance for late night escapades with Charis. Tonight, it would once again be used for a similar function.

Nerissa inspected it to make sure it would still be sturdy enough to hold her weight. After all, she had grown a bit since the last time she had scaled up and down it. Satisfied with the stability of the makeshift ladder, she left the secluded corner and followed a stepping-stone path to the main area of the gardens.

Rows of glow lamps had been neatly arrayed in the sunshine to soak up the daylight so that they could provide illumination after sunset. Most people didn't even think about how glow lamps worked. They gave light in the darkness, and that was all that mattered. To Nerissa, though, it was her curiosity about this very phenomenon that had ignited her desire to learn more about how the world around her worked. Charis must rue the day that she had volunteered to sneak in a book about how glow lamps were made. It had been the first in an unending stream of clandestine texts.

Nerissa spent the remainder of the morning in the gardens helping to position rose garlands and answering a multitude of questions. All the while, her mother sent frequent messages telling her to go and rest. Finally, the last minute preparations were complete, and she was able to slip away to fetch her second costume from the dressmaker's shop.

By the time she returned, it was mid-afternoon, and her stomach was growling. In all of the rush, she had forgotten to eat breakfast and lunch. She stowed the hanging bag containing the costume, along with the boxes containing her shoes and mask, in the back of her wardrobe and went down to the kitchen for a late lunch. There were only a few hours remaining before the festivities would begin.

She opened the doors to the kitchen and found the place in an uproar. Pan and his wife, Addy, were there and had already begun to set up lavish displays of pastries. It seemed, however, that the preparations were not proceeding smoothly.

Addy chased a stumbling Pan, waving a rolling pin in one hand. "Stop this foolishness right now, Pan! Oh! What were you thinking? There's so much work to be done!"

Pan continued to run, ducking Addy's swings with the pin and merrily chuckling the whole way. "I had to try the wine to see if it was fit for drinking, my sweet. One can never quite be sure! Especially considering it was made by that sour old grape."

"I am not a sour grape! The nerve!" scoffed the shriveled-looking winemaker from the corner. Nerissa had to disagree with Pan. In her opinion, his wrinkled appearance combined with his perpetual scowl made the winemaker look more like a sour raisin.

"Well, I'll admit that the ones you used for the wines definitely weren't sour. They were delicious!" Pan's cheeks were rosy as he toddled around the corner of a table, grasping the edge to stay upright.

"Of course they were!" Addy and the man yelled in unison. Pan grabbed handfuls of flour from a nearby bowl and threw one fistful after another toward the two of them. It was an utterly futile tactic, but it caused an involuntary giggle to escape from Nerissa.

It was at that exact moment that Pan noticed her taking in the scene from the safety of the doorway. "Hello, Neriss-OW! That hurt!"

Pan's temporary distraction had given Addy time to catch up and clobber him from behind with the rolling pin. He sat down on a nearby stool and whined, rubbing his head. A dent in his puffy white hat marked where Addy had inflicted the blow.

"I'm sorry you had to see that, Nerissa," she apologized, still tapping the rolling pin on her open palm and glaring down at Pan menacingly.

Nerissa chuckled. She grabbed a flour-dusted apple from a basket of fruit on the counter as Addy continued. "His mother warned me that I'd need to take up the rolling pin if I married him. I thought she meant so that I could share his passion as a baker, but I've since come to learn otherwise."

"You know you love me." Pan's voice was small as it drifted up from behind a white cloud.

Addy looked down at him with one eyebrow raised, visibly holding back her amusement. "Oh, I do. Sometimes I don't know why, but I do."

Nerissa didn't bother restraining her laughter. She held the apple in her upraised hand as she waved farewell to the group and left the kitchen. One day she hoped to be as happy with someone as Pan and Addy were with each other.

# 6

## MASQUERADE

*Nerissa*

Nerissa returned to her room to find that the maids had prepared a bath for her in the short time she had been in the kitchen. A small kettle of water had also been left behind on the hearth, its steam heating two rows of metal hair curlers. But those weren't the only things that had been delivered. There was also a tray on her bed with a tea kettle and a small jar of honey.

She opened the folded piece of paper accompanying the tray, and inside she found her father's firm, square handwriting. The honey was the freshest batch from the farm and would help with her allergies, he wrote. In smaller print at the bottom, he had added that the tea would taste much better than the medicinal herbs her mother planned to send later. She smiled as she laid the card back on the tray. The last thing she wanted was to have to choke down a wretched mixture of medicine.

"Thanks for the warning," Nerissa murmured. That was just like him. Her mother knew how to make her feel better outside, but her father knew how to make her feel better inside.

After closing the balcony doors and barring the hall one, she rolled the steam-heated curlers lock-by-lock into her hair and secured them with U-shaped pins. Then she poured herself a cup of the tea—making sure to add a generous portion of honey—and sank blissfully into the rose and strawberry scented bathwater.

More than a half an hour passed before she could summon the willpower to climb out. Even then, she only managed to do so because the teacup was empty and the bathwater was growing progressively colder. Reluctantly, she swaddled herself in a dressing robe and sat down in front of the vanity mirror to apply her makeup and unwind the curlers from her hair.

Instead of shaking out the resulting mass of curls, she restrained them in a beaded black net that was held in place at the base of her neck by two shimmering combs. Hopefully, the curls would hold until later. Her reflection stared back at her from the mirror, and Nerissa smiled, satisfied. Even her less than ample chest was satisfactory tonight, now supported by an incredibly uncomfortable corset. Sometimes it was necessary to suffer for beauty.

No sooner had she donned her dress and mask than the distant sound of music and the din of festive voices began to filter into the room. She hastily grabbed a piece of stationary from her desk and scribbled the message she would later give to her mother, saying she was retiring early. After tucking the paper securely into the back of the dance book on her wrist, she hurried down the corridor to join her parents in front of the double doors leading to the main hall. The party had begun, and the time for the hosts to make their entrance was close at hand.

"How are you feeling?" her mother asked.

At the same time, her father said, "You look lovely!"

Nerissa smiled. Her mother and father were a perfect match, as elegant and regal looking as always. "I'm feeling better than before—thanks to your tea and honey, Father."

"Did you take the medicine I sent you?" her mother asked.

"Medicine? No one brought me any medicine," Nerissa replied. She tried to look like this was the first she had heard of it being sent to her.

Rica gave her husband a suspicious look, but he feigned innocence and shrugged.

Rica sighed and took his arm as the doors to the great hall opened slightly. A graying man poked his head through the gap.

"We are ready," Rica said.

The man nodded and pushed the doors open fully.

"Presenting Rica, the Blood of Chiyo's past; Parlen, the Bond of Chiyo's present; and Nerissa, the Heiress to the future of Chiyo," he said while speaking into a hollow metal cone that amplified his voice so that it would be heard even by those at the back of the room.

In past years, Nerissa had forced herself to smile as she descended the stairs a few steps behind her parents. Tonight, however, her lips were curved upward into a genuine smile in anticipation of the festivities to come. She held her chin high and surveyed the opulent surroundings.

The preparations of recent days had transformed the hall into a glittering spectacle. The two massive chandeliers that normally went unused were now adorned with hundreds of glow lamps. They cast soft rays of light around the room through their beveled glass panes. More lamps hung from ironwork sconces mounted to the wine-red wall. Diaphanous crimson fabric draped in billowing swags between the pairs of tall stone columns that lined the path leading from the staircase to the ornate double doors on the opposite side of the hall.

Nerissa joined her parents at the foot of the stairs where they were already engaged in conversation with a man dressed in a dizzying costume entirely composed of tiny black and white checkers. Beside him stood a young woman wearing an outfit even more garish than her companion's. It was possibly the most scandalous outfit Nerissa had ever seen.

The dress was composed of nothing but layers of peacock feathers! The skirt was shockingly short, and the neckline plunged deeply enough to reveal an immodest amount of cleavage. Just looking at the woman made Nerissa feel embarrassed and, if she were totally honest, a tiny bit envious. Ironically, her mask covered every inch of her face except her eyes and lips. Foot-long feathers extended ostentatiously above her head and out to each side.

*What designer would ever have made such an audacious outfit?* Nerissa wondered.

"Nerissa, this is Governor Akkub of the city of Silvus and his daughter Darci," Rica said. Her mother's countenance was completely unruffled, as if she were oblivious to the pair's obnoxious outfits.

Nerissa had not yet mastered that level of diplomacy. She wasn't sure that she ever would.

"Welcome, Akkub and Darci," Nerissa said. She concentrated on looking directly into Akkub's eyes, fearing that she might become dizzy if she looked at his checkered mask for too long. She turned to Darci and smiled graciously, only to receive an unctuous smirk in return. Nerissa found herself taking an instant dislike to the feathery hussy.

Much to her relief, it was then that the orchestra conductor announced the first dance of the evening was about to begin. With fast-paced music and dance steps that involved switching partners frequently, the opening dance traditionally served as an ice breaker. The idea was to put each person in contact with many new faces. There would be barely enough time to dance a few steps together and share a few brief words. It was the perfect opportunity to make an escape from Akkub and Darci without being rude.

Akkub held out his arm. "Would you like to dance, Heiress?"

Nerissa accepted, and they stepped into the forming circle of dancers.

"If I am not mistaken, Silvus is the region immediately south of Rhea. You must have traveled quite a distance to attend tonight," Nerissa said as the dance began. She had barely finished her sentence when her foot was crunched beneath one of Akkub's missteps. With every passing moment, she liked the governor of Silvus and his daughter less and less.

"I would not miss such an exciting night for anything, Heiress," he replied smoothly. The words themselves were innocuous, but Nerissa had the distinct impression that there was something else implied in them. Whatever chance she had to elucidate their deeper meaning though was lost as the beat swept her into the arms of her next masked partner.

She whirled between faces of feathers and rhinestones, dogs, more birds than she could count, bears, and even a fox as the music continued. The multitude of smiling masks gradually blurred together until there was no distinction from one to the next. Just when she was beginning to tire, the song ended and the musicians transitioned to something softer and blissfully slower.

There was little time to rest though. Nerissa stepped away from her last partner, and a swarm of eligible bachelors materialized by her side. Normally, she would have strategically turned down most of them in an attempt to avoid being subjected to their fawning and superficial praise. Tonight, she gladly accepted all of the invitations since she knew that she would not be fulfilling the vast majority of them. Once the dance book had circulated to each young nobleman in the group, there was not a single blank line left. It seemed that the Heiress was expected to dance non-stop the entire evening.

Time passed by swiftly, song after song, partner after partner, making each passing second more precious than the last. Nerissa flipped through the pages of her dance book and was relieved to discover that the night wasn't even halfway through.

*One more dance, and I will be free,* she thought as her next partner approached.

"My dearest fiancée, you look ravishing tonight," the Dalmatian gushed.

Nerissa's smile eroded as she realized who it was behind

the mask. Dallin was the son of her mother's dearest friend, so they had spent many summer afternoons together as children. At the tender age of seven, Nerissa had made the unfortunate mistake of promising to marry him. A promise he had apparently taken to heart, heedless of her protests that no rational person would consider promises made at age seven to be binding. In her opinion, her pseudo-fiancé was potentially more obnoxious than Darci's and Akkub's costumes.

"I am not your fiancée, Dallin," she said, straining to keep her voice pleasant. Her father had always said that persistence and tenacity were traits to be admired in a person, but Nerissa was pretty sure that Dallin was an exception to this rule.

"There's no need to be coy with me, darling," he gushed with a wink. "You recognized me right away. That proves we have a special kind of bond."

"Well, there is no one else quite like you," she said. Did he really think anyone else would have the audacity to refer to her as their future wife?

"So you finally admit that you hold me in special regard?" His voice held such earnest hunger that it sent chills crawling down Nerissa's spine.

"I stated a fact, nothing more and nothing less. I am not going to marry you, Dallin. We are only friends, in case you've forgotten. And we'll be less than that if you continue making such absurd statements," she replied. Nerissa was reaching the limits of her tolerance, yet Dallin seemed blinded by his infatuation. It was time to make an escape before she lost her temper.

"You'll see someday that I'm the ideal man for you. We are a perfect match! We love so many of the same things:

roses, archery..." He paused, straining to think of more of their allegedly numerous common interests.

"Yes, we have *so* many things in common," she said dryly.

An image of Dallin serving as an archery target and human pincushion crept unbidden into her mind. "Now that isn't such a bad idea," she murmured, so wrapped up in her fantasy that she didn't notice she had spoken out loud until it was too late. Biting her bottom lip, she prepared herself for the worst.

"I knew there was hope! I will let nothing come between us, Nerissa!" Dallin's exclamations continued on. He was probably planning their wedding and choosing the names of their children, but Nerissa was only vaguely aware of his babbling. She had just spotted a chance to get away. Darci was heading right toward them. As far as Nerissa was concerned, there wasn't a more perfect person she could pair with Dallin.

She wrenched her hand from his grip and waved. "Darci, there is someone here you simply *must* meet!"

Darci smiled broadly as she approached. The feathers protruding from her mask, along with various other "bits" of her, bounced with each step. Nerissa quickly introduced the two and then excused herself under the pretense of needing a bit of air.

Not wanting to waste another minute, she approached one of the footmen standing attentively at the bottom of the staircase. She handed him the note she had written earlier and instructed him to deliver it to her mother as soon as possible.

By the time the footman had disappeared into the crowd, Nerissa was already up the stairs and halfway to her room. She did not pause until the bedroom door was closed and barred behind her. Leaning against it briefly to catch her breath, she relished the feeling of coolness on her back imparted by the door. The great hall was a broiling maelstrom of movement and sound compared to the quiet stillness of her room.

A moment later, the wardrobe doors rattled as they were flung open with unbridled excitement. The hook on which her second costume hung was so far inside the massive wardrobe that Nerissa practically had to climb into the closet to reach it. She emerged, treasure in hand, with a triumphant grin and untied the protective cloth bag.

She petted the soft fabric of the feathered dress affectionately. In the past, the masquerade had been a magical night filled with masked faces, fantastical costumes, and glittering lights. Anything seemed possible, and even the most mundane became surreal. Yet, since her acceptance as Heiress, it had turned into one more obligation to be fulfilled. This night would be different though. Thanks to this costume, tonight she would finally be able to enjoy the masquerade the way she had in the past. It was ironic that she could only truly be herself when she was pretending to be someone else.

Wriggling out of her white dress and into the orange on her own was no small feat, but Nerissa managed it without ruffling too many feathers. The dress itself was even more beautiful on her than it was on the hanger. The fabric floated down to the floor in elegant orange folds. The skirt, divided into two crisscrossing layers above her knees, left her bare lower legs visible among the swirling sunset-colored layers. The back of the dress was accented with feathers, extending from either side like a pair of wings. While her earlier dress had been embroidered with the image of the mythical phoenix, this dress truly made her one.

She turned away from the mirror and fetched the boxes containing the mask and her shoes from the wardrobe. After setting them on the vanity, she removed the shoes from the top one and slipped them onto her feet, winding the ribbons up her leg before tying them off in a long-tailed bow just below her knee. The backs of the shoes were also adorned with feathers to match the dress. She inspected herself in the mirror and grinned with satisfaction.

Nerissa then hastened to retrieve the tiny barrettes from the window sill where she had left them that afternoon, and her smile widened upon noticing the way that the skirt flowed back from her feet with every step. Dancing would truly be enjoyable without constantly having to worry about tripping over the hem. With the box of barrettes in hand, she twirled around, spinning and swaying all the way back to the vanity table.

*I'm not acting like a giddy little girl,* she told herself as she plucked the phoenix ring from her finger and dropped it into one of the drawers. *I'm merely warming up for the night ahead.*

She paused to release her hair from the beaded net, and locks of golden-brown ringlets cascaded down her back. To her great relief, the spiral curls from earlier had indeed held. She tousled them with her fingers and pinned her hair back from her face, fastening the remaining barrettes randomly throughout the rest of the unrestrained locks.

One final touch remained before she could return to the festivities, and Nerissa eagerly pried away the lid of the box containing it. The mask was covered in feathers that had been dyed the same sunset color as her dress. Its edges were decorated with elegant gold scrollwork, and rhinestones accented the eyes. Feathers fanned out on either side, mirroring the wings on the back of her dress. It was not unlike Darci's mask, but the look was elegant rather than gaudy.

Returning to the full-length mirror, she slipped the curved stems of the mask behind her ears like she would a pair of glasses and pulled free an errant strand of hair that had become tangled among the feathers. She then stuffed the boxes and dress bag back into the wardrobe and turned her attention to the bed. If anyone came in to check on her, she wanted them to think she was asleep, so she mussed the blankets and shoved pillows beneath them to give the appearance that it was occupied.

After shuttering all of the glow lamps, she went out onto the balcony and scanned the gardens to make sure she would not be seen. Her fears of being spotted were unnecessary, however. Since the balcony was on the far side of the gardens from the party, there was no one around.

She clambered down the rickety trellis, silently praying that it would hold and wary of the thorny vines merely fractions of an inch away from snagging the delicate fabric. Somehow she reached the bottom with both dress and skin unscathed—and the trellis intact. It was a wonder on all accounts.

Treading carefully across the stepping-stone path, she peeked into each window she passed with breathless excitement. Still, despite her enthusiasm, she hesitated upon reaching the tall doors. This was the moment of truth. Would she be recognized in spite of all her efforts to hide her identity? If so, she would lose her one opportunity for a night of freedom and end up having to explain her behavior to her parents. Even worse, what if she were completely ignored? It would confirm her belief that she was only noticed by people because she was the Heiress.

With a deep breath, she pulled the door open and submitted herself to the clamor inside. No one turned or acknowledged her as she entered. It was an unusual, but pleasant, occurrence—one that gave her time to truly take in her surroundings. While she had admired the decorations earlier, it wasn't until now that she realized exactly how beautiful they were.

There were so many details she had taken for granted, like the expansive carpet she now stood upon. It was plush and crimson-colored, trimmed in gold thread. So beautiful, but trod upon by hundreds of feet with little appreciation. Candles inside tall marble vases were scattered throughout the room to provide extra illumination. The vases were surrounded by garlands of sparkling glass beads and red roses.

Nerissa had grown those roses herself in the greenhouse specifically for this occasion. She wondered if anyone else had even seen them or if they were taken for granted too. Beauty was expected here, rendering anything less unacceptable.

With no obvious place to go, Nerissa made her way to the sprawling tables laden with food. People milled around the area, talking and laughing with cups of wine or cider in their hands. Some had a rosy blush to their cheeks, so it seemed that Pan was not the only one who had enjoyed the spirits a bit too much tonight.

Nerissa was hovering near the dessert tables, having just finished eating one of Pan's strawberry tarts, when a young man dressed as a Dalmatian suddenly grabbed her free hand.

"Would you care for a dance, my lady?" he asked, sweeping into an impossibly low bow. "Or has your book already been filled for the evening?"

"I-I-I," she stammered, her eyes wide. Of all the bad luck, apparently Dallin could find her on instinct alone. "I arrived a short time ago." It was all she could think to say.

"Don't worry. It is but one dance, and I'm certain that my fiancée wouldn't mind. She is not the sort of woman who gets jealous, no matter how hard I try." He winked playfully as if to say his fiancée's lack of jealousy was a measure of how secure their relationship was. Could he truly be so blind to the fact that she wanted him to turn his tender attentions toward someone else?

Unfortunately, in this case, the "someone else" he had selected was none other than his so-called fiancée in disguise. Nerissa said nothing. She simply couldn't find the words. She was beginning to fear that they truly did have a special connection, albeit one-sided. It was a decidedly unpleasant thought.

"Please don't be overwhelmed because I am the future Bond of Chiyo. I know it may be intimidating for a lesser noble like you to dance with someone like me." He prattled on, no doubt regaling her with tales of his future title and glory, but Nerissa had stopped listening.

She was horrified to see this side of Dallin. If he acted this way toward everyone, the whole capital must believe they were engaged! The temptation to set him straight was rapidly beginning to rival her desire to remain anonymous.

"Pardon me, but may I cut in?" asked a young man from behind a hawk mask. "I simply cannot wait any longer to share a dance with this exquisite beauty."

Without waiting for an answer, he smoothly slid between Nerissa and Dallin, taking her hand and steering her deeper into the crowd. Dallin was left behind, slack-jawed, still trying to figure out what had just happened.

"You had the look of a woman in need of rescue," the hawk said, looking down at her with mischief sparkling in his lazuline eyes.

Nerissa remained silent, still taking in this stranger. She didn't remember seeing anyone in such a mask earlier in the evening. He certainly had not been one of the men to request a dance from her.

"At least, it appeared like you wanted to get his paws off of you. Was I wrong?" His voice was warm and sounded sincere, but the mischievous twinkle in his eyes remained. "If I'm mistaken, I will gladly escort you back and make my apologies."

"No!" Nerissa exclaimed. That had come out more forcefully than she had intended. "I mean, thank you for rescuing me, as you described it." There was something about him she liked. Maybe it was his eyes. "I'm not sure I am any safer in your clutches though," she teased.

He wrapped his arm a bit tighter around her waist as they moved in step with the music. Those blue eyes now were filled with both mischief and mirth. "Yes, well, birds of a feather should stick together," he quipped. "Besides, it's sort of my job."

Nerissa pursed her lips in mock anger. "Are you making fun of my costume?"

"Not at all. You, my lady, are the most remarkable creature here," he crooned.

"You know how to lay the charm on thick, don't you?" Nerissa grinned and changed the subject. "I don't think we've met before."

"Well, that would be a difficult thing to say for sure, considering that we're both in disguise," he replied soberly. "In truth, I *am* sure we have never met before. I would never forget those eyes of yours."

"I meant that I don't remember having seen you here earlier in the night," Nerissa clarified, glad that the mask hid her reddening cheeks. She was getting flustered and absolutely did not want him to see her blushing.

"This is my first time attending the masquerade, but I've been here since the beginning of the evening," he replied with an ambiguous smile. "You, on the other hand...I thought I heard you say you had just arrived."

He was sharp. Nerissa's lips twisted to the side wryly. "I have, in a way."

The music stopped temporarily, and they paused to join in a round of applause with the rest of the crowd. Nerissa noticed that her partner's arm had briefly lingered around her waist before clapping. She felt her cheeks warming again and forced herself to take a deep breath. What came next, now that the song was over?

"Would you like another dance?" she asked.

He reached out to take the new dance book that braceleted her wrist. "I wouldn't want to have to rescue you from that puppy twice in the same night."

Stunned, Nerissa watched as he slid the tiny pencil from its clip, opened the book, and proceeded to write his name on every line. He paused, noticing her stare.

"Am I too bold?" he asked.

Nerissa shook her head firmly. "Not at all. I'm told that fate smiles upon the bold."

She tilted her head to read from the dance book more easily. Instead of writing the name of his costume, he had written his own name! Since this was his first time attending the masquerade, could it be that he didn't know the custom? Or had he done it intentionally?

"Is that so? It seems I'll always have fate on my side," he said, his voice thick with mock arrogance. At least, Nerissa took it for mock arrogance.

"What manner of bird is a Rian anyway?" Nerissa asked. She couldn't resist teasing him a bit.

Rian laughed and shook his head. "This practice is new for me, so it seems that I am the boldest—and apparently a very foolish—sort of hawk."

Just then, the first notes of the next song slowly rang throughout the room. Rian clasped Nerissa's outstretched hand, and the pair began to dance again.

"Now that we will be spending the remainder of the evening together, Rian, what family are you from?"

A frown flickered across his lips, passing so quickly that Nerissa almost thought she imagined it. It was replaced with another of those mischievous grins.

"That's a secret," he said. "After all, if you know who I

am, what is the point of a disguise?"

Nerissa threw back her head and laughed, watching the room spiral around them. "You make an excellent argument! I should remind you that I *already* know your name."

"Since you know *my* name, is there something I can call you other than 'my lady'?" he asked, laughing with her.

"What would you like to call me?" Nerissa asked.

The beat of the music picked up as the song reached its climax. There was no opportunity to talk now. Keeping up with the rhythm of the drums required their full concentration. Soon they were spinning so fast that the colors in the room seemed to streak together. Reds and yellows blended with her orange dress like flames swirling around them.

As the last notes of the song played, Rian spun her one last time and then swept her back. He held her so close that she could feel his warm breath against the nape of her neck as he supported her arched back in one cradling arm. Nerissa was fairly certain that the room was still spinning even though she knew they had already stopped moving.

"To answer your question, I'd like to call you by your name, of course," he whispered in her ear.

Nerissa was suddenly acutely aware of his hands. They were firm and strong as they clasped hers but were also soft and gentle. She shook her head in an attempt to regain her senses. No matter how nice his hands were, she wasn't going to fall prey to his charms again. She had charms of her own, and it was time to turn the tables on her mysterious hawk.

A mischievous smile spread across her face. She backed away and waggled one finger at him, laughing as she melted into the crowd. "If you know who I am, what is the point of a disguise?"

# 7

## A ROSE AMONG ROSES

*Rian*

The amused smile vanished from Rian's face as his partner turned away with a pert smile and disappeared into the crowd. Surely this coy little phoenix was only teasing him and not actually leaving him here. But after a moment passed with no sign of her return, he had to admit to himself that she was not coming back.

Rian snapped his mouth shut, just now noticing that it had been hanging agape. "No one gets the upper hand on me," he said, diving into a fleeting gap between dancing couples.

This was his first assignment in the capital. So far, the evening had been much more interesting than expected. It had been nearly twenty years since Casimer's failed attack, and if he were going to attempt an attack again, he would have done it long ago. Still, being chosen for duty at the masquerade was an honor and a great responsibility for Rian and his cohorts.

The pair of orange wings he sought flashed a few feet ahead of him, bobbing out of sight again as a couple whirled past. With a frustrated sigh, he waited for another gap to appear. After dodging out of the path of a pair of twirling bumblebees and ducking in time to avoid knocking a tray of glasses out of a servant's upraised hand, he finally reached the edge of the crowd. Unfortunately, now there was no sign at all of the wily phoenix.

Scowling behind his mask, Rian slammed his open palm against the wall and then resumed scanning the room for any sign of her. Realistically, it would be far easier to find another partner to help speed the evening along, but he had no interest in anyone else now that he had met this girl. The phoenix had his full attention. She had captivated him from the second he saw her hovering next to the dessert table, and he didn't want her to slip away.

"She's playing hard to get..." The words had barely left his mouth when he was suddenly jostled from behind.

"Please pardon us," said the man who had run into him. The swirls of tiny black and white checks on the man's suit made Rian feel like his eyes were crossed.

"Quite alright," Rian grunted, but the man and his scantily clad peacock companion had not bothered to wait for a response. They were already continuing on their way toward the doors. *Why were those two in such a hurry to leave the party?* Rian wondered. *And where has my nameless phoenix gone off to?*

Right when he was about to give up hope, he spotted the pair of feathered wings again—this time near the tall doors leading to the gardens. A minute later, the doors opened, and Rian followed quickly behind.

He stepped onto the patio, where the gurgling of water could be heard as it cascaded over rocks at the edge of the gardens. Ripples of light shimmered from below the water, which was illuminated by submerged glow lamps. A gentle wind rustled the leaves of the surrounding trees, causing the light from the glow lamps nestled within the branches to dance across the ground. Somewhere in the distance came the haunting call of a loon.

In the midst of it all was his phoenix, watching the sun set behind the mountains that loomed on the western horizon. She stood with her hands clasped behind her back, innocently, expectantly, while the last saffron rays of the sun framed her in a luminous halo. Locks of her hair and the feathers on her mask and wings danced in the breeze like hundreds of tiny flames. Here, she truly was a phoenix. She had enthralled him without speaking a single word or even giving him so much as a glance. As he approached, she turned to face him, a beguiling smile playing across her lips.

Rian pried his eyes away from her, pretending to examine a garland of roses draped around one of the two tall stone pillars. "Beautiful," he said under his breath. She drew up beside him, and he noticed the twinkling of tiny glow lamps that had been woven into her hair. He didn't know why such a small detail would impress him so much, but it did.

"They are, aren't they?" she said, reaching out to pet the velvety petals of the flower nearest her.

"What?" he asked, confused. Then it occurred to him that she must actually have overheard him and mistakenly thought he had been talking about the roses. This was his chance to turn on the charm. "I mean, some are definitely more beautiful than others."

He scanned the length of the garland and spotted a rose

with its petals spread wide and covered in dewy pearls. It was unusually large and stood out among its peers even in the twilight. Only this one was suitable enough for her. He plucked the rose from its place and offered it to her.

"Anyone can spot a rose growing among weeds," he said. "But few can see the extraordinary rose among roses."

"It does take a keen eye to find the one that is different from all the others when they are so similar." She looked up from the rose and smiled at him gratefully. "I saw this one earlier. It almost seems a waste of its beauty to mix it so indiscriminately with the ordinary-looking roses."

Rian's eyes locked with hers. "You know, I'm not just talking about roses," he said.

But before he could see her reaction, the ornate doors connecting the gardens to the grand hall flew open, admitting a man disguised as a fox to the garden. Long tendrils of pure white hair arced behind the newcomer as he strode toward them, and Rian exhaled in annoyance.

He knew the face hidden behind that mask—it belonged to his best friend, Raysel. Raysel was supposed to be leading the groups patrolling the festivities outside the Manor. If he was here, it meant that something must have gone wrong.

Raysel greeted the phoenix with a bow and then addressed Rian. "I need to speak with you."

"How did you find me out here?" Rian asked, still feeling a bit peevish.

"I followed you through the crowd," Raysel said with a shrug of his shoulders. "It's not like it was difficult to do."

The phoenix snorted in amusement, earning her a

quizzical look from both men.

"There is an urgent matter that needs your attention. *In private*," he added forcefully.

Raysel then turned to the phoenix. "My Lady, I would advise that you go back inside where it is safe. I have no doubt that your absence will be noticed shortly."

"Thank you for your concern," she replied. A hint of bewilderment tinged her voice.

With duty demanding his attention, there was nothing else for Rian to do. He grabbed the phoenix's hand and lifted it up to brush with his lips. "I hope to see you again soon. Will you wait for me? You still owe me a few dances." With an impish grin, he swept into a low bow and departed without waiting for her response.

"How kind of you to ask," she murmured, her eyes narrowing as the two departed. She twitched her lips to the side thoughtfully and spun the stem of the rose between her fingers. Leaning back against one of the tall stone columns, she said to no one in particular, "I suppose I can wait a *little* while."

———————◆———————

Rian and Raysel's rapid footsteps rang out from the marble floors, shattering the silence that consumed the empty hallway. The corridor was devoid of both life and light, but they ran heedlessly through the darkness with the confidence of those intimately familiar with their surroundings. Halting in front of an antique tapestry, Raysel pulled it aside to reveal a small door hidden in the wall. Inside lay two swords, the last of the many that had been hidden there earlier.

Raysel tore away his fox mask and sent it clattering

carelessly to the floor. A look of relief flittered across his face as he picked up Thorn. Rian followed suit, pulling the beaked mask from his face before retrieving his own sword, Dragon's Bane. He felt the same sense of relief to be holding his blade again. This had been the one night he could not keep it with him since swords would have drawn unwanted attention. Yet it had seemed unnatural not to have Bane by his side.

"You said there was an urgent matter, so what is it?" Rian asked. Raysel's behavior made it abundantly clear that something serious was going on, but Rian couldn't help feeling a bit irritated to have his time with the phoenix interrupted.

Raysel gave Rian a withering look and then turned and ran further down the hall. "I'll explain as we go. Unusual movements have been observed near the river. In addition to that, one of the street patrols reported hearing the cry of a loon from the direction of the docks. It was out of place since loons don't live south of Silvus. It seems suspiciously like a signal of some sort, and we've heard it several times now, so I sent the rest of the group ahead to scout."

Rian nearly tripped over his own feet as realization struck him. He, too, had heard the loon earlier, but he had been so preoccupied that the detail slipped past him.

Raysel continued on, ignoring Rian's misstep. "I approached the docks to investigate and found many men moving around on the decks of two of the boats. It looked like they were moving large objects around. And I don't mean shipping crates. There are no deliveries scheduled to arrive tonight."

They stopped, and Raysel slowly pushed open the heavy wooden door used by the servants to bring shipments in from the docks. He turned to Rian and put one finger to his lips, motioning for silence. The two crouched low to the ground and crept slowly toward a stack of haphazardly piled crates.

"The boats are from the nobles who traveled from the north to attend the masquerade, right? It would make sense that they'd have servants and crewmen staying on board," Rian whispered.

A loon crooned again into the night, this time much closer than it had been in the gardens. Raysel's brow furrowed upon hearing the sound, and his face took on an eerie calmness. It was the same face Rian often saw when they sparred together. The pair rounded a corner to discover two of their companions already taking cover there.

"Look," the closest one murmured. He swore an oath under his breath, but he clutched his bow confidently.

Rian snatched the lenses and gazed through them, searching through the night. Although it was difficult to see clearly in the dusky light, from this vantage he could make out the outline of a catapult on the deck of one of the ships. Stacked up nearby were huge spheres, and a man appeared to be pouring something onto them. Flames suddenly sprung up from lanterns and torches all around the deck, bobbing as the ships creaked and groaned.

Rian's heart sank into his stomach. "An attack," he said, the words cold and stone-like on his tongue. "Where are the others?"

"They are already in formation awaiting our signal," Raysel replied.

Rian nodded, already calculating their next course of

action. The attackers had to be stopped before their plans could be put into motion. If his group could move quickly enough, perhaps it wouldn't be too late to prevent this disaster. Rian drew his sword, hesitating only briefly.

"One of us needs to go back inside and report this to Einar," he said.

"I already warned him on my way to find you," Raysel said.

As always, Raysel was one step ahead. Rian was completely confident that Einar and his men would protect the Royal Family. There should not have been another thought in his mind as a flaming arrow shot into the air and he and his peers poured from their hiding places. But, for one fleeting moment, before instinct took over, his mind flew back to the phoenix waiting for him in the garden.

# 8

## THE PHOENIX TAKES FLIGHT

*Einar*

Einar dodged through the crowd, moving against the flow of dancers to reach the garden doors. He had to see for himself what was happening at the docks. His two fellow guardians were watching over Rica and Parlen in his place, while another of the Ohanzee was stationed outside Nerissa's room.

Meanwhile, the party continued on, the revelers unaware of the impending danger. They milled about, sipping their drinks and chattering as if nothing were out of the ordinary. There was no time to warn them. The guests' safety was, unfortunately, secondary to that of his primary charges—the Blood, the Bond, and the Heiress.

As he approached the garden doors, he saw a woman through the glass panes. She removed her mask, straining to look at something in the distance. Einar's eyes widened in recognition and dread. Nerissa shouldn't be in the gardens. She was supposed to be asleep in her room. That wasn't even the costume she had been wearing earlier.

The building suddenly shook violently, and the crowd around him gasped in unison. The world seemed to stand still. Einar tore off his mask and struggled forward, unceremoniously shoving aside lords and ladies to reach Nerissa. She was so tantalizingly close, just seconds more and he would be there to keep her safe. He watched helplessly as a ball of flames flew through the sky toward them. The building trembled again, and people now began to run. They pushed against each other, desperate to get outside.

Nerissa turned toward the doors as one of the balls struck, and the column she had been standing in front of exploded. Einar ran to her, only to be forced back as the roof covering the patio collapsed, burying the area—and Nerissa—in the rubble.

The metallic clash of swords rang out from behind, somehow standing out over the din, and Einar spun to find Rica and Parlen engaged with a group of costumed revelers. No, those were no revelers. They were Senka in disguise! One of the Ohanzee already lay lifeless on the floor. As Einar watched, Parlen took up the fallen guardian's sword and swung it with futile strokes to defend his wife. All three fought frantically, yet soon they were pinned with their backs against the wall.

Einar longed to aid them, but the wheel of fate was already in motion. A chasm of time and distance lay between them, so great that no man had hope of spanning it. The sword tumbled from Parlen's hand and clattered to the floor as his attacker gained the upper hand. At the last moment, Rica's head turned away from her attackers, and she gave a hope-filled glance to the doors at the top of the shattered staircase. Einar watched, in agonizing impotence, as his comrade and the two rulers were murdered before his eyes.

The building shook again as it was repeatedly pounded by the balls of fire. Flames licked and raced up the strips of red fabric draped in front of the windows. Dust from the shattered walls created a fog that enveloped the entire room, while fire rained down from bits of cloth and wood that had once been decorations crisscrossing the ceiling. Even the panicked screams of fleeing guests were muffled by the seemingly constant thunder of the relentless attack. The once glorious Royal Manor had been reduced to chaos in a matter of moments.

Einar knew who Rica had been thinking of when she looked to those doors. She must have thought Nerissa was in her room and hoped her daughter was safe. He had to get into the gardens. Perhaps Nerissa *was* alive. If he could get outside, there may be a chance to save her. He broke open the nearest window with a chunk of fallen stone and leaped through it, heedless of the flames that threatened him.

Debris littered the area, but the fire consuming the Manor made it easy for Einar to see while he clambered from one pile of debris to another. Miraculously, Nerissa was not difficult to find. She lay partially buried at the very edge of the rubble, covered in dust and blood.

Somehow, the largest of the stone fragments had not landed on her. Mere inches separated the crown of her head from a massive block of the column that had once supported the garden patio roof. The ground around her was splattered with scarlet, and Einar's heart sank as he reached down to wipe off a splotch that marred her pale cheek.

To his surprise, however, his hand met not with the sticky

touch of blood, but rather with the velvet softness of a rose petal. He brushed it away, and it fluttered to the ground. Looking more closely, he could see that the other splatters were petals as well. The broken stem of the flower was still in Nerissa's hand.

Einar scrabbled to remove the surrounding debris, unflinching even as his own hands began to bleed. He gingerly pulled away a blood-stained chunk that had apparently caused an injury to the side of Nerissa's head. The head wound was troubling, but it seemed she had no other major injuries.

With the rubble cleared, she was now free except for her long hair, most of which was pinned beneath the large boulder. Einar knew she treasured her hair, but there was no time to wait for help and no safety to take her to in the city. That left only one choice.

Even without his sword, Einar was never unarmed. "You will have to forgive me, Heiress," he said. He pulled a knife from the inside of his suit jacket and cut off her hair.

He then lifted her up and draped her limp body over his shoulders. The stables were located at the far end of the property, at the edge of the forest that led to the mountains. It was there that he ran as quickly as he could manage, hoping the stables were untouched by the attack.

Fortune had granted them one mercy this night and caution another. Though the horses were skittish from the noise and activity around them, the stables were undamaged. Einar's horse, Wind, stood calmly in the last stall, already saddled.

Einar knew it was always wise to be prepared for a quick departure. His sword and saddle bags, packed with a change of clothing and extra supplies, were on the floor outside the stall—right where he had left them following the morning archery lesson. He pulled an extra blanket from the tack room and wrapped it around Nerissa before mounting Wind.

After settling her into the saddle in front of him and cushioning her head against his chest, he rode out of the stables heading west into the forest, watching and hoping that no one was following. He held Nerissa's limp body with one arm while urging the horse onward with the other.

Even though there was not a single cloud in the sky, it began to rain. There was no other explanation for the water that poured down Einar's cheeks. He wiped the water away, but it continued to fall no matter how hard he wished it to stop. Setting his jaw defiantly, he ignored the burning sensation in his throat and urged Wind on.

He would ride until they were far enough away that it was safe to stop and treat Nerissa's wounds and change her from the tattered dress. With raindrops still rolling down his face, he rode as fast as he could to the one who could care for her injuries, to safety, to home—to Darnal.

# 9

## PROOF

*Casimer*

Sunlight streamed into the room through the open windows, interrupted occasionally as a mote of dust swirled through. Yet even the springtime brightness did not improve Casimer's mood as he impatiently paced the room. It had been seven days since his men had taken Chiyo, and their full success was still unconfirmed.

"I don't understand why you are so anxious, darling. Everything went according to plan," Echidna said. She appeared relaxed, reclining against a pile of pillows on the chaise, but her bracelets tinkled against one another as she repeatedly ran her hands over the perfectly pressed folds of her skirt.

"Nothing is certain until we have the indisputable proof in hand," Casimer snapped. That answer should have been obvious.

His wife made her irritation at his snippiness abundantly apparent by tapping her nails on the wood trim of the chaise.

Casimer could tell that his current behavior was annoying her, but she was the one who had insisted on waiting with him. Still, he forced himself to stop pacing and instead stared blankly at the empty fireplace.

So far, the people of Niamh had been stubbornly resistant to the change in control. The majority refused to even acknowledge him as their new ruler. Their obstinance had been expected, particularly because the change was recent, but swift action was necessary in order to firmly establish his hold.

Unsurprisingly, crime had become rampant as a result of the initial chaos associated with the attack on the Manor. It was only human nature to take advantage of such a situation. Looting and vandalism were the most common offenses. Casimer didn't find the crime level to be of great concern. His men would have no difficulties restoring the peace. It was the vandals that he viewed as most problematic. They almost exclusively targeted postings of his decrees, and suspiciously, there never seemed to be any witnesses. Such public displays of dissent would have to be put to a stop—immediately.

Casimer twitched as Echidna purred softly in his ear. He had been so lost in thought that he hadn't noticed his wife's approach—or even that the tapping had ceased—until she spoke.

"If you have so much extra energy, I know a way to put it to good use," she said, wrapping a lock of his raven hair around one of her fingers." Ladon's been asking for you for days now. No child should be without the attention of his father for so long. You should go spend some time with him, and I will send Nils to you when he arrives." She pointed out the open windows to the sunlit courtyard where their young son was playing under the watchful eyes of his nursemaid.

114

"Nils could be hours away," she added.

Casimer briefly considered her argument and then nodded in agreement. It was sometimes hard to resist his wife's persuasive powers. She could be very convincing when she wanted, and in this case, she did have a point. Hearing his son's playful laughter never failed to bring a smile to his face.

It was then that a knock resounded through the room. The satisfied look disappeared from Echidna's face, and she flopped back onto the pillow-covered chaise with a vexed sigh as Casimer flung open the door.

On the other side stood the very man they had been waiting for. The Chief of the Senka was tall and muscular, and even more devoted than he was brawny. Loyalty was good, in Casimer's opinion, but Nils' dedication was somewhat overzealous at times.

Twenty years ago, his wife and infant son had gone missing just weeks before the tragic accident that claimed the lives of Casimer's first wife and son. Nils' only comment on the matter had been that they'd argued, and she threatened to leave. Beyond that indifferent statement of fact, he seemed utterly unconcerned about their whereabouts.

If the situation had been reversed, Casimer would have turned Renatus inside out to find his family. Had he not seen the shattered remains of their carriage protruding from the waves at the bottom of that steep cliff, he may not have believed his own family was truly gone. That had happened twenty years ago, but the painful memory still felt like a sword through his heart.

"I have the proof you have been waiting for, my King," Nils said. He dropped smoothly to one knee without waiting for a greeting. In his outstretched palm lay a lumpy silk pouch.

Casimer snatched the pouch and untied the knot that held it closed. Three heavy golden objects spilled out into his palm, and he examined each in turn with the utmost scrutiny. He had seen the first two many times on Rica's and Parlen's hands during diplomatic meetings. The rings that the Blood and the Bond wore were instantly recognizable. The third ring, however, was one that he had never seen. The Heiress had not yet been named the last time he had met with the rulers of Chiyo, although it was presumed that their daughter, Nerissa, would be given the title.

He turned the ring over in his hand, and the red gemstone eye of the phoenix glimmered in the bright sunlight. For a moment, it seemed as if the bird were glaring at him accusingly. Casimer shrugged away the feeling. His actions had been justified. What he had done was necessary for the future prosperity of *both* kingdoms.

"I obtained two of the rings from the corpses of the Blood and the Bond myself, my King. We finally found the third ring among the ashes of the Heiress' bedroom. The fire was most intense in that area, so little more than stone and metal remained where it was found," Nils' voice trailed off, letting his silence imply the rest.

"The rings are proof enough," Casimer said. He snapped his fingers closed around them, feeling their weight as he shook his fist triumphantly. "They were worn by the Blood, the Bond, and the Heiress at all times. Wherever the ring found its resting place, so did she."

Echidna laughed and clapped her hands in a rare display of unreserved merriment, and Nil's face split into a toothy grin.

Casimer dropped the rings back into the silken bag and tied the delicate strings. After slipping it into his pocket, he settled into the tall chair opposite his wife.

"Have there been any new rumors?" Echidna asked, having already regained her aloof composure. Even though she appeared to be more interested in examining the tips of her shiny red nails, Casimer knew her better than that. She prided herself on being his eyes and ears. It was a rare occasion indeed when something slipped through her vast network unnoticed.

Nils hesitated before answering, his grin slipping away. "No *new* rumors, my Queen."

Echidna's eyes flicked away from her hand, and she sat straight up in the chaise, knocking some of the dainty pillows onto the floor in the process. "By your emphasis, am I to understand that you have an update on an old rumor? Well? Do not make me ask twice!"

"Have patience, my darling," Casimer enjoined. "Has Nils ever failed to tell you all you wish to know?" Nils bowed his head slightly in gratitude. "Since her body has not been found, there is a rumor circulating that the Heiress is not really dead. Some even say that she used a crystal to escape the fire." Nils almost laughed at the last bit. Echidna did laugh.

Casimer, on the other hand, found very little humor in the news. That strange rumor had to be silenced. It would do no good for the people to cling to some irrational hope that their former rulers would magically reappear. Nothing good ever came from spreading false hope. Not that any rational person would indulge in such fantasies, anyway.

As for escaping by using a crystal? The idea was preposterous! It was yet another example of the fool's paradise that Chiyo had become, fraught with superstition and wild fantasies about crystals and mystical energy. He would not allow anything, even something as far-fetched as that concoction, to undermine his control.

"Have you gotten any information on the activities of the Ohanzee?" Casimer asked.

"There has been no sign of them so far. We've also seen no evidence of their involvement related to the current resistance. It seems they have retreated to their hidden stronghold, wherever *that* is," Nils replied.

"I know that you would like to start looking for the Ohanzee right away, Nils, but there are other matters that must be attended to first. Prepare your men. We have much work to do. I thought that removing the Royal Family would be sufficient to take over control. If I must also wipe the memory of those three from Renatus to make the transfer of power clear, then so be it." Casimer's voice grew more heated with every word. He would save the people of Chiyo from their backward customs, and one day they would recognize and appreciate his actions. The time had come to lead all of Renatus into a bright future, filled with reason and flourishing with knowledge.

# 10

## MEMORIAL STONES

### *Charis*

Charred and broken wooden beams creaked and groaned, shifting precariously beneath Charis' unsteady feet as she picked her way through the haphazard piles of debris. Although it was difficult to see where to step in the darkness, she feared being caught more than falling, so the light from the single open shutter on her glow lamp would have to suffice.

This area was strictly off limits to anyone other than Casimer's workers. It was a fact that Charis was well aware of, but even that could not deter her. Those scavengers were here every day, searching and sifting the rubble for anything of value. Whatever they found was sent back to Casimer, apparently as spoils of his conquest.

To Charis, the idea was more than distressing—it was infuriating. It felt like they carried away a piece of her friend with every item. She had not come here looking for anything specific. All she wanted was to ensure that no more of Nerissa's belongings fell into Casimer's hands. Any of her friend's possessions were precious to her, regardless of their monetary value.

Just ahead of her, climbing high above everything else, was the crumbling staircase. A little over a week ago, Charis had walked up these stairs carrying her weekly delivery of books to Nerissa, as she had countless times before. Now, instead of leading to Nerissa's room, the stairs led to the open sky. The ethereal beauty of the stars seemed out of place above the broken remains. *Is Nerissa among those stars now, looking down from the heavens?* she wondered. From this angle, it looked like it would be possible to climb the stairs and step into the heavens to join her.

Charis steeled herself to press on. Nerissa's room had been on the second floor, but the supporting pillars had collapsed, and the entire level had tumbled to the ground with them. Little remained recognizable, so she scanned the rubble intently in the dim light. She needed to find something familiar that would mark a suitable starting place. The treasures she so earnestly sought could be anywhere, but there was not enough time to look through everything.

A prickling sensation rolled down her spine as she realized that she may also come across something she did *not* want to find. The bodies of those who had perished in the attack should already have been removed and put to rest. Surely, Casimer's men had found everyone by now. However, according to the rumors, Nerissa's body had not yet been found. The sole proof of her demise that had been discovered was her phoenix ring, and that was no proof in Charis' mind. After all, she was the only one Nerissa had told of her plan to switch costumes during the party. Nerissa would have taken off the ring when she changed, but there was no way Charis would share *that* information with anyone.

Had the attack occurred before or after Nerissa swapped costumes? Could she have survived and somehow escaped? Charis hoped from the bottom of her heart that she had.

All other thoughts were banished from Charis' mind when something off to the left caught her attention. There, silhouetted by the moonlight was an unmistakable form. Two thick iron pillars, with a network of curving metal connecting them, jutted sharply out from the rubble. Not long ago she had been sitting on that very bed talking about books with Nerissa. Her search would begin there.

Charis had been digging fruitlessly through the debris for several minutes when a ray of moonlight caught on something small and shiny in a nearby mass of rubble. Her heart skipped a beat with excitement as she plunged her hand into the gloomy nook and retrieved the object.

The abrupt movement caused the wooden beam supporting her to shift. She dropped the glow lamp and tumbled backward in a cloud of dust. Ignoring the burning desire to rub her throbbing bottom, Charis picked up her lantern and opened her clenched fist to inspect her find.

Attached to the blackened crystal in her hand was a fine wire, which had become entangled in a jumbled mass with the stone's six companions. For a moment, Charis could only stare in amazement. These crystals had been one of Nerissa's most cherished possessions! To find them whole and unbroken was even more than she'd hoped for. They had always looked so delicate and seemed so fragile. It was astonishing that they could survive an assault that had reduced the entire Manor to rubble.

Suddenly, a firm hand clamped down on her shoulder, and Charis shrieked with panic.

"Shh! Here, take this." The person's voice was surprisingly gentle in contrast to their grip.

Charis whirled around and found Amon standing behind her, his cloak and long red scarf stirring in the night breeze. In his outstretched hand, he held a handkerchief.

"Th-thank you," Charis stuttered, taking the silken cloth from his outstretched hand. She turned away again and proceeded to rub the soot from the crystals.

Amon leaned over her shoulder in an attempt to see what it was she had found, but Charis quickly enfolded the stones in the cloth.

"What are *you* doing here anyway?" she asked, her shock turning into annoyance.

"I saw you leaving the house and decided to follow you," Amon said. He squeezed Charis' forearm. "It was past curfew, and it isn't safe to be out alone at night, so I was worried about you. This place is off-limits, not to mention dangerous. Let's go before we get injured or someone sees us. We could both get in a lot of trouble if we're caught here."

"I can go anywhere I want, anytime I want!" Charis argued. "There is no curfew in Niamh."

"Casimer rules Chiyo now," Amon replied patiently.

"Only if we let him," Charis scoffed.

Amon's hand twitched, but his expression remained calm. "You would do well to think about who you are talking to."

"And exactly what will you do about it?" She yanked her

arm from his grasp. "You would also do well to remember *your* position. Do you think you would be able to continue your studies if I told my father you threatened me? I know you're up to something. And whatever it is, I'm sure that you can't afford to lose your position at the university."

Amon sighed. "I didn't mean for it to sound like a threat. I'm getting angry because you're being stubborn. The curfew is for our own good. The city isn't as safe as it once was."

The sound of approaching voices startled them both, and Amon dropped smoothly to the ground behind some nearby debris, jerking a lock-kneed Charis down with him. Three men passed by, unaware of their presence. They stopped some distance away, in what used to be the Memorial Garden of the Manor. Slowly and simultaneously, two pairs of eyes peeked over the top of a pile of splintered wood.

There were no trees surrounding the area where the men stopped, leaving them eerily illuminated by the moonlight. Charis had never seen anyone like them before. Long, dark hair swung from high ponytails as the men repeatedly swung heavy mallets against the memorial marker.

The towering obelisk they were destroying had served as the tribute to the Royal Family for as long as Chiyo had existed. The names of generations of Chiyo's rulers had been inscribed there so that the memory of their beloved rulers would be preserved forever. Miraculously, the memorial had survived the attack with little damage. Nerissa, Rica, and Parlen's own names had recently been carved into the tablet at its base. With every swing of the men's mallets, the stone cracked and fragments crumbled away. Each blow tore apart the last and most sacred memorial of the Royal Family.

Charis closed her eyes and slid back to the ground, clutching the folds of fabric inside her pocket as silent tears streamed down her face. Casimer was destroying anything and everything that remained of the people who had been like a second family to her. She felt wretchedly small and helpless, huddling there as the sound of stone breaking echoed around her.

Amon knelt down next to her and awkwardly pulled the hood of her cloak over her head. "Wait here. I'm going to approach them. Once I'm sure they aren't looking this way, I'll take off my scarf. When I do, head straight out the gates as fast as you can." He offered a hand to help Charis up.

"You're going to get in trouble," Charis warned, wiping her cheek with the back of one hand.

"You'll get in far more trouble than I will if you're caught. My uncle will forgive me for breaking curfew, but he would not be so lenient on you." Amon paused a moment, then added, "Be careful on your way back."

Charis looked at him skeptically, and then a thought occurred to her. Why did she care if he got caught? If he did, then he would be gone from the university and she would be rid of him once and for all. The idea should have seemed appealing, but, oddly, it wasn't. She nodded to him in response, still a bit thunderstruck by the whole situation, and Amon patted her once on the top of her head before standing.

He approached the trio with a casual wave, and Charis heard them greet him by name in response. She watched with trepidation as they smiled and chatted casually, the burliest of the men laughing and leaning on the handle of his downturned mallet. It appeared they knew Amon. It wasn't terribly unnatural for King Casimer's cronies to know his nephew, was it? She wouldn't be surprised if they were also involved with whatever nefarious plans he had at the university.

She continued watching until Amon pulled his scarf from his neck and draped it over his arm. Then Charis turned away from the men and ran, keeping her eyes focused on the gates.

———◆———

Charis did not look back, so she didn't see the look of bewilderment and relief on Amon's face as he surreptitiously watched her leave. Nor did she hear the burly man say, "That's enough small talk. You're late. You do have the information, don't you?"

"Of course I do. Have I ever let you down?" Amon replied. He removed the envelope from his pouch and handed it over. "There's no way I would let anything—or anyone—interfere with our plans."

# 11

## THE HIDDEN CITY

### *Einar and Nerissa*

High within the Western mountains, in a city long hidden from the rest of the world, frost shimmered in fleeting moonlight that peeked in and out from behind passing clouds. More than a month had gone by since the first day of spring. The nights should be growing warmer, yet a light glaze of hoar still coated the budding greenery.

Einar's breath came out in misty puffs as he walked toward the small building that served as the place where he and the other two Chiefs of the Ohanzee, Haku and Hania, held private meetings. This was certainly an unusual night, but everything had been unusual since he had returned to Darnal with Nerissa unconscious in his arms. No one in the village— aside from the chiefs and their wives—even knew that Nerissa was the one he had rescued that night. Those who witnessed his return had seen the short remnants of her hair and the spare clothing he had replaced her dress with and assumed that she was a young man. By mid-morning the following day, the whole village was rampant with speculation about the young man's identity.

And until Nerissa awakened, there was no reason to correct their misconception.

"Is that you, Einar?" came a voice from within the trees. A twig snapped nearby, and Einar turned in time to see Jin, Hania's apprentice, emerge from the shadowed canopy.

"Good evening, Jin," Einar replied. "Are Hania and Haku here already?"

"Yes, they're both waiting for you inside." Jin rubbed his arms in an attempt to keep warm and then tilted his head to peer over Einar's shoulder with a look of concern. "Ildiko isn't with you? I've never seen you come here alone. She hasn't had another of her attacks, has she?"

"Ildiko is well, but she would appreciate your concern. She stayed home tonight to care for a patient," Einar answered, deliberately opting to give a vague reply. Even though Jin had already been named as the Chief Advisor's apprentice, he would not be privy to all of the information the three chief's shared until Hania resigned.

Jin's eyes widened and an eager grin crept across his face. "Ah, yes—the young man you brought back with you on the night of the attack. He's going to be named as the new Heir of Chiyo, isn't he?"

"You know I'm not going to answer that," Einar said. He glanced around, scanning the area for any sign of Haku's wife, Ebba. She must be somewhere nearby, watching to keep curious villagers from getting close enough to overhear the chiefs' meeting. "More importantly, shouldn't you get back to your rounds? Or is Ebba on guard duty alone tonight?"

"Alright, alright," Jin relented, heaving a long, misty breath of disappointment. "I look forward to the day when I can join the three of you. I feel useless not being part of the discussions." He pounded one fist into his open palm. "But if *I'm* not allowed to hear your conversation, then I'll make sure no one else does either."

---

"There were fifty Senka? Rian should consider it fortunate that all of his squad returned alive," Haku said, the fire in his voice growing with every word. His unnaturally white hair swayed side to side as he shook his head for emphasis.

Hania nodded sagely, his expression as placid as Haku's was animated. "Rian is still young. Right now, he feels the pain and loss of failure more acutely than his wounds. I expect that he feels an even greater responsibility because of his father's role in the attack."

"He has no control over his father's actions. Particularly those of a father he doesn't know," Einar said. "As for his own part in the fight, his squad was grossly outnumbered. No amount of training or years of experience could have helped in that battle. Rian will come to realize this eventually, and his pride will heal over time. Until then, we will ensure that he is kept too busy with training to become absorbed by self-pity." Einar's voice was strong, but the dark circles under his eyes belied the weariness that lay just beneath the surface.

"Rian is the least of my concerns!" Haku's brown eyes narrowed and frustration colored his face as he continued. "Casimer has held Niamh for the greater part of a month, and we have done absolutely nothing about it!"

Hania quashed Haku's growing vehemence with a stern

look. "Save your fury for later, Haku. We have much to discuss tonight." He slid his gnarled hands into opposite sleeves of his robe, and he paused, frowning. "According to our informants, Casimer has been in contact with the governors of each province asking for their allegiance. The Governor of Silvus was the first to submit—five days after Niamh fell."

"I never did trust Akkub," Einar muttered under his breath.

Haku folded his arms across his broad chest and shot Einar a knowing look. "What of the other regions?"

"I've had no word from the more isolated regions outside the influence of the provincial capitals." The wrinkles softened a bit as Hania suppressed a smile. "But I have heard something quite interesting from the mountain province of Rhea."

"If they refused to cooperate with Casimer, it would be a great relief! Rhea spans all of northern Chiyo...I don't want to think about what our situation would be like if Rhea chose to side with Casimer," Einar said.

Hania's eyes twinkled with amusement. "I was told that Governor Alden covered Casimer's messenger in honey and feathers and chased him back to his carriage. He told the man that if he didn't hear him clucking all the way out of the city like the chicken his king was, he would have him thrown into the coop with the other fowl birds."

"A waste of good honey," Haku remarked dryly. "They may need our help later."

"That's unlikely," Einar interjected. "Rhea is surrounded by the Yoshie River. It is so deep and swift that it is impossible to cross except at the two drawbridges. Even before now, the region was nearly independent. Casimer would be hard-pressed to take Rhea by force, especially considering how poorly he has been able to keep the rest of Chiyo in order thus far. That is why he's asking for the governors' help. He doesn't have the power to do it alone—yet."

Hania held up one finger in a cautionary gesture. "We should be careful not to misinterpret Alden's actions as loyalty. He is bold, charismatic, and impetuous all at once. He is quite a...," he paused, searching for the right word, "colorful...man, like his father was. He is also like his father in that he acts only in Rhea's best interests. Relations between Rhea and the Royal Family have always been good, but Alden knows they could just as easily stand alone as remain part of Chiyo."

"Fantastic," Haku groused. "Tell me that you, at least, have good news, Einar."

Shadows hid Einar's eyes as he stared down at the floor in front of him. "Nerissa's wounds are healing, but she still sleeps. Ildiko is doing everything she can. She's using both herbs and crystals and even talks and sings to her."

"So Ildiko continues to have hope that Nerissa will wake?" Haku asked pointedly.

"Yes," Einar replied.

"That is enough for me," Hania said, his voice and expression untroubled.

"Then should I request that Nerissa's name be left off the memorial tablet? The replacement for the monument Casimer destroyed is almost complete," Haku said.

"Let it be placed in the Ohanzee cemetery with her name on it," Hania said after a moment's consideration.

"Why?" Einar challenged, finally pulling his gaze away from the floor to meet Hania's eyes.

Hania's calm exterior melted away, replaced by resignation. "Nerissa is not the first one who has fallen into such a sleep. Not everyone wakes from it, and the longer it lasts, the less likely it is that she will. While I don't like to think of the possibility, we must not let our wishes make us lose focus on reality. Everyone thinks that the Heiress perished with her parents in the fire, and they mourn the loss of all three. If we reveal that she still lives, they will be elated, but if she dies without awakening, their sadness will be redoubled. It is far better not to give back hope prematurely."

Haku threw his head back in exasperation. "Is there nothing else we can do other than sit back and watch Casimer steal all of Chiyo?"

"Haste could cost us more than patience right now. We should continue with our current stance until the next course of action becomes clear. There is a reason for all chaos even though it may not be immediately apparent." Hania's words hung in the air as silence descended upon the room.

———————◆———————

Nerissa was floating in a dream, a place outside of time, on the horizon of life and death, where fantasy and reality blended together. It was a place of limitless possibility which could only be reached when the body rests and the mind's eye opens, freed from the restrictions of thought and reason. She drifted in the dream, her vision clouded and hazy, but she felt unconcerned as long as she could see the soft light that shone like a beacon in the distance. Nerissa ached to move toward it, yet something tied her down and prevented her from reaching the serene light that seemed so tantalizingly close.

Perhaps it was the pain that anchored her down. Why *was* there so much pain? The thought no sooner drifted through her mind than it evaporated into the fog. All that remained was the knowledge that if she could reach the light, everything would be fine.

A voice, melodic and soothing, wove through the silence. It reminded her of the lullabies her mother used to sing. Nerissa recognized the melody, but the words were oddly muted. As she strained to hear better, she lost focus on the beckoning light, and the pain pulled her down into the darkness below. The dream faded, and her eyes fluttered open, flooding her senses with another kind of light.

Nerissa closed her eyes again, shying away from the blinding sunlight that streamed in through a window a few feet over the bed. She was content to listen to the singing, now clear and sharp like the ringing of tiny bells.

Despite the pain, she felt warm and safe here. She opened her eyes to see tiny rainbows scattered across the ceiling, fading away and reappearing as the sunlight dimmed and intensified. She looked for her crystal chimes, and a feeling of disorientation washed over her when she didn't see them. For that matter, there shouldn't be a window or a wall next to her bed. *Her* bed had a scrolling framework and tall poles, not a plain wooden board near her feet.

There was only one possible explanation. The rainbows didn't come from her crystal chimes because this was *not* her room.

"Where am I?" she rasped, her throat rough from weeks of disuse.

"Oh!" The voice that answered her had a musical quality to it, even when not singing. "You're awake!"

The woman dropped the plate she had been scrubbing back into the soapy basin with a clatter and hastily grabbed a nearby towel to dry her hands. She was frail and impossibly thin, with skin whiter than the palest cream, but she moved gracefully and easily across the room. Her hair was tied back at the base of her neck with a simple white ribbon. It shimmered like fine strands of gold and silver in the sunlight as she leaned over to drag a short stool closer to the bed.

"You are in my home in Darnal. My name is Ildiko," the woman said.

"Darnal? I know all of the cities in Chiyo, and I've never heard of such a place," Nerissa croaked. At least, she didn't remember having heard of Darnal. Her mind still felt too muddled to be sure.

Ildiko lifted a carafe from the small table next to the bed and poured a glass of water. "Here, have a drink." She pressed the cup to Nerissa's lips until she managed to take a sip.

"Of course you haven't heard of it. Darnal is the hidden city of Chiyo." Ildiko's tone was utterly serious. Although her lips quirked upward at the corners, the suppressed smile failed to push away the dolor in her large gray eyes.

"How did I end up in a 'hidden' city I've never even heard of?" Nerissa asked. She reached up to rub her aching temple and found a cloth dressing between her hand and the source of the pain.

"Now *that* is a long story—and one best saved for later," Ildiko replied. She gently pulled Nerissa's probing hand away from the wound. "There is someone who will be overjoyed to see you awake. Many people, actually. Before that though, how do you feel?"

"My mind feels foggy. What is going on? How did I get hurt?" Nerissa felt foolish and a little afraid for having to ask such questions. She should know how she had been injured, but for some reason she could not recall.

"You don't remember how it happened?" Ildiko's lips formed into a thin line when Nerissa shook her head. "Well, some time and proper food should clear out that fog. You do remember who you are, right?"

"Of course." Nerissa scoffed at the thought. How could she not know who she was? On the other hand, she couldn't remember how she had been hurt, so perhaps it was a fair question. "I am Nerissa, Heiress of Chiyo, daughter of Rica the Blood and Parlen the Bond."

"If you can remember that mouthful, you are fine," Ildiko said. She sounded relieved though her eyes remained sad. "Let me make you more comfortable."

Ildiko helped Nerissa to lean forward and adjusted the pillows so that she could recline on them in a semi-upright position. "Alright then, I'm going to go get him. Try not to move too much. I will be back shortly."

She was already halfway to the door when Nerissa called out to her. "Please wait! I apologize. You obviously know who I am, so we must have met before, yet I can't remember who you are. Are you a doctor?"

"That is because we have *not* met before, but you have met my husband," Ildiko said, smiling kindly as the words danced from her tongue. "As I said earlier, my name is Ildiko. I am Einar's wife and a practitioner of medicine. Hold the rest of your questions for a moment. I'm going to get Einar." She bowed with the grace of a swan and then disappeared into the adjoining room.

Ildiko had said she was a practitioner of medicine, so that explained why she was caring for Nerissa's injury. Nerissa wondered how she had come to be here though. Why wasn't she being cared for in Niamh?

While that thought was still in her mind, Einar burst into the room, several seconds ahead of his wife. He stopped short and stared at her with an unreadable expression, as if he were suddenly unsure of what to do.

"Einar?" Nerissa's voice was thick with surprise. Ildiko had said her husband's name, but it hadn't occurred to Nerissa until now that this Einar and her strict archery instructor were one and the same.

Einar let out a choked laugh and hurried to the stool Ildiko had occupied earlier. He took Nerissa's hand, squeezing it excitedly. "You're alright! Well, not exactly...but you're awake, and that's good enough! I don't know what I would have done if you had died t—"

"Einar!" Ildiko exclaimed, cutting off the end of his sentence. "The poor girl has just come back to her senses, and you seem to have lost yours in exchange."

Nerissa tried to laugh. The blanks in her mind were discomforting, but seeing a familiar face, no matter how out of place it may be, made her feel somewhat better. "I've never seen the Einar I know act this way. It's hard to believe that the person in front of me is my all-seeing archery instructor."

Ildiko winked impishly as she helped Nerissa to drink some more water. "Do you feel up to having some broth or porridge?"

"Not really. I feel like my stomach is hollow, but maybe food would resolve that," Nerissa said. She poked it experimentally a few times to be sure it hadn't *really* become hollow.

"I think you're right," Ildiko said with a nod. "Einar, we've run out of rice. Can you give me a hand bringing some up from the cellar?"

"Of course," he said. He hesitated before letting go of Nerissa's hand. "We'll be back in a few minutes."

Nerissa listened intently until their footsteps ceased a short time later. They had either gone to another room without opening a door or they had stopped for some reason. Her parents had used that same maneuver many times when they were discussing something she wasn't supposed to hear.

A dark suspicion in the back of her mind told her that she already knew what that reason was. There was no other explanation why *Einar* would have been the first person to see her instead of her parents. Nerissa eased out of the bed onto wobbly legs and shuffled across the room one teetering step at a time. It was of the utmost importance to be quiet, so she couldn't afford to let herself fall. Fortunately, she had only to reach the doorway for their voices to become clear.

"What were you thinking, mentioning her parents right away?" Ildiko scolded in hushed tones.

"You're right, Ildiko. I wasn't thinking. I realized it as soon as I spoke," Einar replied. "She is going to ask about them soon. I'm surprised she doesn't already suspect something is wrong."

Ildiko's empathy for Nerissa was obvious in her voice. "It's inevitable, but for now, let's not tell her anything unless she brings it up first. She needs time for her body to heal. It would be cruel for her to find out too soon."

"It would be even crueler not to tell me and let me imagine all the horrible possibilities instead," Nerissa said.

Both Einar's and Ildiko's expressions were the essence of surprise as their heads swiveled simultaneously toward the doorway where Nerissa leaned against the frame.

"I want you to tell me what is going on, and I'd really appreciate it if you told me everything."

Einar helped Nerissa return to the bed, promising with each step that he would tell her exactly what had happened. She was certain she knew why her parents weren't there but found that her eyes were surprisingly dry. Across the room, Ildiko began boiling water to make rice porridge.

Einar wrung his hands together, looking as if the news he was about to deliver caused him physical pain. "Do you remember the masquerade?"

Nerissa thought back, focusing all of her concentration on recalling anything about the masquerade. Despite her efforts, she could not remember a single event that had happened after leaving Tao's house the night before the ball. Even those memories seemed fuzzy and distant. "No, I don't have any memory of that day at all."

Einar sighed heavily, his countenance laced with sadness. "Casimer attacked the Manor during the masquerade. His men launched balls of flames at the Manor from a boat docked on the river. Even though you were supposed to have retired to your room for the evening, I found you in the gardens under a collapsed pillar. That is how you were injured."

Listening to his description of the night's events gave Nerissa an eerie feeling. She could recall her carefully constructed plans in detail: make an appearance at the dance, feign illness and retire early, and then return wearing her second costume to enjoy the night in blissful anonymity. Based on Einar's story, she must have followed through, but it seemed that fate had other plans for that night.

"What about my parents? Were they injured as well?" she asked. "Is that why you haven't sent for them yet?"

"Nerissa..." The look in Einar's eyes as he said her name was an external mirror of the heaviness that Nerissa felt inside. "I don't know a gentle way to say this," he said, folding and refolding his hands in his lap. "They were assassinated by Nils, the Chief of the Senka, and a group of his men. I saw it all." Einar's voice wavered, but he continued on. "I was blocked by debris, so there was no way to reach them in time."

He paused, waiting for a reaction from Nerissa. When she said nothing, he continued on, telling her about the Ohanzee and their role as the secret protectors of the Royal Family of Chiyo, and about the Senka, their counterparts in Marise. He described how he had rescued her and brought her to Darnal. The explanation took quite some time, particularly with Ildiko's insistence on interrupting to make sure Nerissa ate a few bites of the rice porridge she had fixed.

Nerissa assumed that Einar must have given her a thorough explanation of who the Ohanzee were and their role as guardians of her family. But, in truth, she heard little of what he said. His voice had rapidly dulled to a distant buzz as the reality of the situation set in.

Her parents were gone. They were not away on a trip, and they would not be returning. They had been ripped away from her. Chiyo, their legacy, had been ripped away from her as well. Casimer had tried to kill her, too. Nerissa's mind reeled in pain, in agony, in anger. Conflicting desires to either hide under the blankets or rush out headlong seeking Casimer for revenge welled up inside her.

"Nerissa?" Einar prodded gently. "It's alright if you are angry. Scream, cry—do whatever you must to feel better. Take as much time as you need to heal and think about what you should do next. You are welcome to stay in Darnal as long as you like. Permanently, if that is what you wish. Know that the Ohanzee will be behind you no matter what you decide. If you want to fight, we will go to battle for you. If you would rather remain here in peace, you are welcome to stay in our home." Einar added hesitantly, "There is no shame in choosing peace."

At that, Nerissa finally broke her silence. "The days of Casimer's rule over Chiyo are numbered, Einar. I will see to that," she murmured. "Thank you, both of you, for taking me into your home and caring for me."

Nerissa hoped she sounded sincere. She really was grateful. It was just difficult to show any emotion at all right now. Einar nodded once before bidding her goodnight, and then Ildiko shuttered the lone glow lamp and extinguished the candles.

"I'll be in to check on you frequently throughout the night," Ildiko said. "If you need me in the meantime, ring the bell next to the bed." She pulled the door closed quietly behind her, leaving Nerissa alone in the darkness.

Thoughts raced through Nerissa's mind as she waited restlessly for sleep to come. She remembered Charis telling her that crystals were shattering all over Niamh. She had even seen one of Tao's break with her own eyes. There was no doubt in her mind that *this* was the change they had foreshadowed. She wished that she had taken the warning more seriously, but how was she to know back then?

Like the crystals, her life and everything she held precious had been shattered into a thousand fragments. While she believed she could rely on Einar and Ildiko, nothing of her previous life remained. Alone in the darkness of a strange new world, she felt the saline sting of unbidden tears as they streamed silently down her cheeks from behind closed eyes.

# 12

## SPRING FLOWERS

*Nerissa*

A few days later, Nerissa sat beneath an oak tree sipping anise flavored tea with Ildiko and Hania. This was the first time she had met the eldest chief, and she had been surprised by Hania's appearance. Nerissa had expected that he would be tough and stern, like an aged version of Einar.

In actuality, Hania didn't appear very chief-like at all. Instead, he reminded Nerissa of a child playing dress up. While Hania's face was a map of wrinkles, it seemed that the creases were caused by the varying degrees of his perpetual smile rather than a disapproving frown. Those around his eyes were the most telling of all. As his smile grew, more and more lines appeared at the corners. Two deep lines ran down from the corners of his mouth, which only added to his childlike appearance by making his chin look like that of a talking doll.

Their conversation thus far had covered a variety of topics. According to Hania, everyone in Renatus believed she had perished in the attack, aside from the three chiefs and their wives. If Casimer learned she was still alive, he would undoubtedly seek her out. Even the slightest hint to the contrary could mean that her friends would be viewed as potential sources of information. Nerissa had a hunch that Casimer would not simply accept their ignorance at face value, and the last thing that she wanted was for anyone to be put in danger for her sake. So she had requested that Hania and the other chiefs keep her true identity a secret for now, even among the rest of the Ohanzee. As much as the choice pained her, it was safer to allow the misconception to persist until she figured out what to do next.

"Your roses are growing quite fast this spring," Hania said, turning the conversation to lighter matters. Nerissa's ears perked up at the mention of roses.

"Yes, at this rate the first buds will open weeks ahead of the summer solstice," Ildiko murmured over the rim of her teacup.

"Indeed," Hania said. The spring flowers have been particularly beautiful this year. I think they become more so with every passing year. Their memory is a comforting promise in the gray winter and a reason not to mourn the falling leaves during the harvest. New blossoms will always grow, even after the coldest winter."

Ildiko frowned as she saw Nerissa's brows furrow together in response to his comment.

"I have something you may be interested in seeing, Nerissa," Ildiko said. She stood and made a point of giving Hania a nettling look on her way to the house.

Hania merely shrugged and turned his attention to Nerissa, his smile unwavering. He gestured with his thumb in the direction Ildiko had gone. "Be gentle with her. She's been sickly since she was born. But regardless of her physical limitations, she is as protective of you as Einar is." The wrinkles around his eyes creased thoughtfully before he continued. "I do hope that I didn't upset you. Sometimes I forget how much age has changed my perception of death."

Nerissa took a sip of her tea and considered her reply. "No, you didn't upset me at all, Hania. As a matter of fact, you reminded me that my mother said something similar to me when my grandfather died."

Hania's smile deepened. "I told Rica the very same thing then. It warms my heart to find that she thought enough of my words to pass them along to you. You know, your parents aren't really gone. They're waiting for you to meet up with them again, just like they waited for you before you were born.

"My late wife is there with them too. I remember that she used to sit at the gate waiting for me to return from missions, years ago. As soon as I was within arm's reach, she would grab my ear and drag me home like a misbehaving child. She may tug them *both* right off my head for making her wait so long this time. Death is nothing to fear. This world is neither the beginning nor the ending."

"You are right, of course. Thank you for the reminder, Hania."

Hania simply nodded in response. They sat in silence drinking their tea until Ildiko returned from the house. She handed Nerissa a small, padded box and then spread the rest of the objects across the blanket in front of them.

Nerissa opened the container and took out the earth-fire crystal within. It was so large that she had to lift it with both hands. She turned the gray-green stone in the sun and watched the light reflect off the multitude of prismatic inclusions.

"This is an amazing collection, Ildiko," Nerissa declared. She gestured toward the array of smaller crystals in front of her. "You said you have never left the village. How did you acquire these?"

Ildiko nodded graciously in response. "There is another member of the Ohanzee, Raysel, who has an even greater affinity for crystals than mine. He brought them back for me to use in healing."

"So that *is* why you had them around my bed!" Nerissa exclaimed. In her excitement, she sloshed a bit of tea out of her cup. "I've heard many stories that mention crystals being used for healing, but there's nothing documented to prove their effectiveness. I've never been able to tell whether the tales were true or not."

"I know from experience that the crystals do help some people. You are a living example of that," Ildiko said, eliciting a questioning look from Nerissa. "By all logic, you should not be as healthy as you are. When Einar first brought you here, I wasn't sure if you would live to see the next sunrise. Yet, immediately after awakening from a four-week slumber, you were able to walk across the room when you should have been too weak to sit up without help. Now, merely a few days later, you sit with us casually drinking tea—and spilling it—with fewer lingering injuries than many of the men who fought that night. I am glad this is so, but the speed of your recovery is nothing short of extraordinary."

Nerissa sheepishly dabbed at the wet ring that had formed on the blanket beneath her cup. "And you think that the crystals are the reason?"

Ildiko nodded in affirmation. "I put them around you only two days before you awoke. Your wounds healed faster in those last two days than in all the preceding weeks. Some may dismiss it as a coincidence, but I will never be convinced otherwise. I wish I had used them right away."

Nerissa reached out and gently squeezed Ildiko's boney hand. "It's alright, Ildiko. There's no way you could have known. Your talents and care are the reasons why I am here today. I owe you more than I could ever repay."

"You are too free with your compliments. I did what anyone in my place would have done," Ildiko replied. Despite her denials, color rose to her pale cheeks as she tried to suppress a proud smile. "Crystals are peculiar. Oils and herbs work the same way for everyone, albeit sometimes to varying degrees, but crystals are not like that at all. Since they are unpredictable, I use them as a last resort. For most, they have no effect at all. For some, they seem to help a little. And, for a very small number, they are extremely effective. In any case, I do the best I can to heal those who come to me, and I will do so by whatever means possible."

"I wonder why that is," Nerissa mused. "I'll have to share your information with Tao next time I visit her." But, almost as soon as the words left her lips, she realized that she would not be visiting Tao anytime soon, and her excitement dissipated.

"If you ever want to talk to someone about crystals, I could introduce you to Raysel," Ildiko suggested.

"I'll keep that in mind," Nerissa said. She tried to sound enthusiastic to hide the dismay that was threatening to fill her heart. "Raysel certainly does have a good eye for crystals. I'm envious of your collection!"

Hania hummed softly to himself at the mention of Raysel's name and watched the sediments swirl at the bottom of his cup.

"A good eye? Yes, you could definitely say he has that," Ildiko said thoughtfully. "Be sure to ask him sometime about the earth-fire crystal he wears around his neck."

"What is special about it?" Nerissa asked, her curiosity piqued by Ildiko's enigmatic tone.

"My description would do it no justice. You'll just have to see it with your own eyes," Ildiko said. "That is, if you can pull them away from his face long enough to look at it. He is quite handsome, after all."

"All this talk of crystals has reminded me of something I heard a long time ago," Hania said abruptly. "I prefer to deal with things that are more tangible, so I tucked it away in my memory but never gave it much thought. It seems like something you might be interested in hearing, Nerissa."

Nerissa leaned forward in anticipation. "Please go on."

"There was a man in Rhea whom I had the fortune of getting to know quite well over the years. Since most crystals come from the caves and hills within Rhea, I would say he was more knowledgeable about them than most people. He told me many marvelous things about those caves and the stones collected from them. Some of his stories were more curious than others, but this was the most remarkable: he claimed that crystals could remember things." Hania's eyes widened, mixed with wonder and skepticism, as he said the last part.

Nerissa didn't bother trying to temper her curiosity. "Remember things? In what way?"

"That was exactly the question *I* asked." Hania chuckled, amused by Nerissa's unrestrained interest. "He only said that sometimes the crystals absorbed energy from events that happened nearby. This caused strange things to occur from time to time. For instance, people reported seeing ghosts or hearing odd sounds. He also said that there were old tales of a 'lost art' that allowed information to be intentionally stored in crystals and then recalled later in exact detail. It seemed to me that he knew more about those stories than he let on, but he said he knew nothing else. When I pressed him, he said he had already shared too much."

"Hania has a knack for getting people to say things that they normally wouldn't," Ildiko said with a sly grin.

"I'll have to keep that in mind," Nerissa commented, tapping one finger against her lips with feigned apprehension.

Hania glowered at them both. "My talents have served their purpose in the past." He sounded cross, but the creases at the corners of his eyes said otherwise.

Nerissa laughed. "Wouldn't it be fascinating to find crystals that contained information about the past? It seems too incredible to be true."

"Fascinating? Perhaps, but history is not always what we think it to be," Hania cautioned.

"What do you mean?" Nerissa failed to see how history could be different from one person or place to another.

"History has a tendency to gloss over details and blur the truth. Not everything that is recorded about the past is what actually happened. For example, your family is said to be direct descendants of Gared, yet that isn't *strictly* true."

Hania's tone was so matter-of-fact that the information seemed like nothing more than a bit of trivia, but to Nerissa the knowledge was quite a shock. "What do you mean by that?" she asked, beginning to feel like she was repeating herself.

"The throne of Chiyo has been passed down through the ages unbroken, with each generation selecting its successor. However, that does not mean the *bloodline* was unbroken. On more than a few occasions, the children of the rulers were found to be unfit for the position, or the rulers had no children at all, so an Heir was chosen from outside the family. That selection was well known at the time, but as I said, history has a way of losing track of those kinds of details."

"If I'm not related to Gared by blood, then can I really be called his descendant?" Nerissa asked.

"Although you may not be related by blood, you are Gared's descendant in the most important sense. It is a simple question of what you perceive to be more significant: lineage or character. You were chosen to be the Heiress because you possess, by choice, the same traits and ideals that Gared himself believed in. Your mother was chosen for the same reason, and her father, and his father before him. You carry on the qualities that separated Gared from the rest of the men of his time. That makes you more closely related than any blood heritage would. Even if the bloodline were unbroken, it would be so diluted by now that you could hardly call it a relation at all."

Nerissa felt like her head was spinning. "Hania, how do

you know all of this?"

"It is written in the records that we keep. The Records of the Ohanzee aren't entirely the same as the histories that you studied at the University, are they?" he asked with a small chuckle.

Ildiko nodded absently in agreement while pouring herself another cup of tea.

"Similar, but not the same," Nerissa said. "Why hadn't I been told about them? Are they a secret?"

"In a way they are. The official histories have always been kept by the Ohanzee. Since our very existence is a closely guarded secret, the records we keep are too."

Nerissa nodded thoughtfully. Hania's logic did make sense. "That brings up something I've been thinking about lately. Who exactly are the Ohanzee? Why didn't I know anything about you until I arrived here? Einar tried to explain everything to me after I woke up, but honestly, I was too overwhelmed to take it all in."

"That's understandable," Ildiko said, squeezing Nerissa's arm.

Hania finished his tea and set the cup on the tray alongside the teapot. "Surely you had seen us occasionally, watching over you from the shadows. Why didn't you ask then?"

"I did ask once," Nerissa replied. "The first time I saw someone in the shadows, it scared me. My parents said that you were guards and they would tell me more when I got older. I knew better than to bring it up again. That was one of many things they had promised to teach me." A trace of anger laced through the loss that filled her voice as she finished.

Hania patted her shoulder sympathetically. "That is your answer. You would have been brought here when your mother stepped down and passed the ring of the Blood to you. In this case, that time came much sooner than anyone expected."

Hania folded his hands in his lap and gathered his thoughts. "As you were told, we, the Ohanzee, are the secret guardians of the throne of Chiyo. Our history can be traced back to the Gullintanni, a group of spies who reported directly to Gared and whose existence was also a closely guarded secret. Originally, our purpose was to ensure that the governors of the various regions of Renatus did not abuse their power. If it was necessary, the Gullintanni members informed Gared and a 'bad' ruler was promptly removed from their station. Our job later expanded to include serving as Gared's personal guardians.

"When Renatus was divided into Chiyo and Marise for Gared's great-grandchildren, the Gullintanni was also divided into two groups: the Ohanzee and the Senka. Over time, Chiyo and Marise grew apart and so did the Senka and the Ohanzee. Although few people know of our existence, our two groups are completely aware of each other.

"Now, rather than being two parts of one whole, we serve opposing sides. Our duties have remained nearly unchanged through the years. To this day, we train vigilantly so that we will be prepared to defend Chiyo. Aside from a few isolated incidents over the years, our lives were peaceful until twenty years ago. The Senka have been trying for decades to locate this city. You see, it would have been much easier for Casimer to usurp your parents if we were no longer in the picture. Fortunately, our location is still a well-kept secret."

Nerissa leaned up against the tree trunk behind her, trying to give her weary muscles a break while taking in everything Hania said.

Upon seeing her fatigue, Ildiko turned to Hania. "I think that's enough for today. Even though Nerissa is recovering quickly, she still needs plenty of rest."

Hania rose. "Very well, but there is still one thing I need to ask her," he said. "I know that you have requested to keep your true identity hidden. However, it will complicate our information-gathering efforts if my successor, Jin, is not in on the secret. Would you find it problematic if he knew your identity too?"

"Since he is your successor, I see no reason to leave him out. I would not want anything to hamper our ability to keep up with the activities of Casimer and the Senka," Nerissa replied.

"Excellent. I will see you at this time next week to give you updates on events in Chiyo." Hania then smiled serenely and followed Ildiko to the gate.

# 13

## THE RECORDS OF THE OHANZEE

*Nerissa*

The solstice was still weeks away, but summer was clearly running ahead of schedule. It was midmorning, yet the air was already oppressively hot and laden with humidity. It was the sort of day where, by noontime, even the most industrious person would have dedicated their efforts wholly to seeking a cool place to languish until sundown.

Nerissa, for one, was actually looking forward to helping Ildiko with the wash this afternoon. Not because she particularly liked doing the laundry, but because splashing in the cool, sudsy wash water would be a welcome—if only partial—reprieve from the heat.

For the time being, she simply did her best to ignore the locks of hair clinging to the nape of her damp neck while Ildiko and Einar chatted over breakfast. Their voices were a distant drone as Nerissa stared out the window longing for home and the constant breeze the river fans provided. Were it not for Hania's weekly updates, she would have wondered if the fans were still standing. Casimer seemed to be quite fond of destroying things—and quite good at it too. The updates, at least, kept her from fearing for the immediate well-being of Niamh and its inhabitants.

It distressed her to learn how Casimer was treating her people. He had imposed strict curfews, and groups of guardsmen patrolled the streets at all times. Gatherings of more than three adults had been forbidden. Such edicts were unheard of before now. The people of Niamh had always been free to go about their lives and follow their own pursuits. Their freedom was unlimited as long as they did not violate the Common Laws, which forbid theft, assault, murder, and the like. They were encouraged to speak out against perceived injustices and even to petition the Blood and Bond directly on matters. Such freedom was the cornerstone of Chiyo's governance, which meant that Casimer's heavy-handed laws were in direct opposition to the ideals ingrained in their society.

*Does he treat the citizens of Marise the same way?* Nerissa wondered.

In spite of his draconian measures, or perhaps because of them, there were rumors of a movement growing behind the scenes to carry out an uprising. Hania had told her there were also rumblings that a second group was quietly attempting to subdue the unrest. He was unclear on who was leading either group. The Ohanzee were not involved, and Hania insisted that there were no indications that the second group was under Casimer's influence. Nerissa agreed with that assessment. Open displays of force were more his style.

She grumbled under her breath at that thought. When Ildiko glanced at her over the rim of her coffee cup with eyebrows raised questioningly, Nerissa shook her head in response. She vented her irritation by dipping her knife into a jar of strawberry jam and scraping it vigorously over a slice of sourdough bread. The heat was *definitely* not helping her mood this morning.

It didn't matter *who* was behind the unknown force. Nerissa sincerely hoped that they would successfully quell the uprising before anything happened. Violence would do far more harm than good to the city.

The only influence she could exert was through agents that Hania was now actively trying to embed in both of the mysterious groups. All information so far indicated that the first group was little more than a poorly organized faction of citizens planning an attempt to physically overthrow Casimer's hold on the city. But no number of farmers with pitchforks or merchant's fists would be able to free Niamh. As much as Nerissa would like that to be possible, his hold on Niamh was too firmly entrenched to be removed without external help. And that help certainly would not be coming.

The two major cities remaining in Chiyo had taken opposite sides. The city of Silvus and its surrounding areas, governed by Akkub, had willingly accepted Casimer's authority almost immediately after Niamh was taken. That was suspicious, to say the least.

On the other side was Rhea and its outlying region, governed by Alden, which had rejected all attempts at so-called diplomacy from Casimer. They were now asserting their independence—with success. Rhea was where King Gared had been born and the historic capital of Renatus. It had always been virtually independent of her parent's authority and possessed a geographical advantage and sufficient resources to resist Casimer indefinitely.

Though Alden would likely be an ally, he would not divert resources from Rhea and risk compromising that advantage. There would be no assistance coming to Niamh until Nerissa and the Ohanzee made their move. She frowned at the thought, disliking the fact that she didn't have any idea what that move should be.

As a leader, Nerissa knew that she should be more concerned about the plight of her people—and she genuinely was. Yet, of all the offenses Casimer had committed, her mind always flew back to one in particular. It was unsettling enough to know that Casimer had prevented the traditional funeral procession and the cremation ceremony for her parents. It would have been her funeral too, as far as most people were aware. Not a day passed that she didn't think of her parents and feel empty inside knowing that she had lost her memories of the last moments spent with them.

It was also not a comfortable feeling to know that her own name was considered among the dead. She already felt like a ghost anyway, hardly even recognizing herself in the mirror. However, Casimer's desecration of the stone memorial statue bearing her name, her parents' names, and her ancestors' names was nearly more than she could tolerate. The destruction of the monument made it seem like their lineage had never existed. As if their memories deserved no respect. A person's body may disappear, but their ideals and deeds allowed their spirit to live on in this world as long as there were those who remembered them. How many names had been lost when the stone statue was crushed?

Nerissa chomped into the slice of sourdough bread she had been holding, roughly tearing away the tough crust with a quick flick of her wrist. A trickle of sweat rolled down the back of her neck as she moved, and she mentally growled. No, the weather was doing nothing to improve her mood.

"Why don't you have some coffee?" Einar asked. "At least the bitterness will give you an excuse to make that kind of face."

The gruff question snapped Nerissa from her thoughts, and she forced a small smile. "I have no idea how you can drink that so early in the morning. Coffee is far too bitter to be paired with anything other than desserts or sweets."

"It's an acquired taste," Einar said, pouring himself a refill.

Ildiko patiently watched her husband add cream to the cup. "You should try it with milk or sugar sometime," she suggested to Nerissa. "Though I doubt that you'll want to use quite as much as he does."

"Humph," Einar said. He paused in the middle of pouring a third heaping spoonful of sugar into the now light-brown liquid, but tiny grains continued to spill over the edge of the spoon anyway.

"I think I'll stick with cold tea," Nerissa replied. "Even if you pay no mind to the taste, I have no idea how anyone can drink something so hot in this weather."

"Drinking something hot makes you feel cooler," Einar said. "Isn't that common knowledge?"

No sooner had the words left his mouth than a knock came from the front door.

"They're here early," Ildiko said, sounding only moderately surprised.

Einar muttered as he left the table, his voice barely audible over the sound of his chair grating across the floor. "Since he came by early, he's probably hoping we'll offer him breakfast."

A few minutes later, the sound of shoes coming off and hitting the wooden floor of the entry way made it obvious that the visitors would be staying for a while. There were two of them, if Nerissa had counted the number of thumps correctly.

"Who is it?" she asked. "I didn't know we were expecting company today."

"You'll see shortly. Their visit was meant to be a bit of a surprise...something to cheer you up. I'll let them explain," Ildiko replied as Einar returned to the room followed by Haku and Jin.

Haku bowed, placing one hand over his heart in a single fluid motion. "Good morning, my Lady Nerissa." His movements were so natural that it seemed he had done them hundreds of times. Then again, Nerissa supposed he must have greeted her parents that same way many times during the twenty years he had spent with them. He straightened and turned to Ildiko. "Good morning to you as well, Ildiko."

Jin also bowed to Nerissa, though he lacked Haku's fluidity. "It's rather hot this morning, isn't it, Lady Nerissa?"

Nerissa chuckled for the first time that morning. "I think that may be an understatement."

"Indeed, and it won't be any better this afternoon!" Jin laughed and inhaled the aromas of breakfast with evident appreciation. "That smells delicious, Ildiko!"

Einar glanced at Ildiko, his expression blank and

unreadable to most, but not to her. Many years of marriage had given both of them the ability to understand the other's subtle cues. Though he said nothing, that look most clearly said "I told you so."

"You're welcome to help yourself if you like," Ildiko replied, sounding amused.

"I couldn't possibly refuse some jam and bread. You make the best strawberry jam I've ever tasted!" The grin slid from Jin's face a second later, and he rapidly added, "Please d-don't tell my wife I said that."

"I wouldn't think of it," Ildiko replied smoothly. She ignored another of those looks from Einar as she slid a plate across the table to him. "Would you like something, Haku?"

Haku smirked and took a seat at the table. "No, thank you. *I* ate before I came."

"I ate beforehand too!" Jin protested around a mouthful of bread and jam.

Haku leaned back and sighed while scratching at his short beard. "Considering the heat, today is a particularly good day to visit that place," he commented.

"What place would that be?" Nerissa asked.

"A place that is always cool, no matter how hot it gets outside," Haku said. "First though, Hania asked us to bring you to his home."

"There is something there that he has wanted to show you," Einar added, anticipating Nerissa's inevitable question. "We were waiting until you had recovered enough to go out."

"Really?" Nerissa looked to Ildiko who responded with a

nod and her usual serene look. "Why not tell me what these mysterious things are now?" she asked Einar.

"It's easier for you to see it for yourself. Under normal circumstances, we would have taken you there after you had been given the ring of the Blood," he explained.

Nerissa knew by now that there was no point in pressing them. Einar and Haku had no intention of revealing either the mysterious "place" or "things" until they arrived at Hania's. Still, that didn't stop her from being curious. The city of Darnal seemed to hold an unending number of mysteries. This was in no small part due to the fact that she had been completely unaware of the existence of this city and its inhabitants until recently.

She had been stunned to learn that, in addition to there being a secret group of guardians for her family, there was also an entire hidden city full of people supporting them. There were those among the Ohanzee who lived as tradesmen: farmers, teachers, artisans, smiths, apothecaries, and doctors. Some of their crafts served dual purposes. The smiths made metalware not only for household use, but also forged weapons of extremely fine quality.

There were others, whose trade was dedicated solely to the protection and defense of Chiyo: spies, archers, swordsmen, and specialists in hand-to-hand fighting arts. The spies often posed as merchants and traded goods made by the artisans in Darnal as a cover for their true occupation. Even more operatives lived permanently within villages throughout Chiyo and sent their reports back via Hania's network.

Every vocation within the Ohanzee fell under the jurisdiction of one of the three chiefs. Einar was the Chief

Guardian. He was the leader of all of the skilled fighters and had also been her mother's personal guardian. Haku served as the Chief Preceptor. He oversaw academics and specialized training for both the tradesmen and guardians in Darnal. Hania, the Chief Advisor, was the leader of all the Ohanzee messengers and informants. He managed a network that spanned the entirety of Chiyo and portions of Marise.

Jin, who was just a few years older than Nerissa, would one day replace Hania as Chief Advisor. At their first meeting, he had laughingly introduced himself as "Hania's errand boy." To watch him now, it was a bit hard to understand why Hania had chosen him. Compared to Haku, Hania, and Einar, he seemed impulsive, capricious, and even a slight bit childish. However, that playful, easygoing attitude belied a cunning and shockingly astute mind. He was able to instinctively filter the truthful grains from rumors and gossip and could readily deduce relationships between bits of information.

Nerissa had learned over recent weeks that Jin's reasoning skills were one of the Ohanzee's greatest assets. When questioned about the seeming dichotomy of his nature, Jin replied that not thinking about trivial matters left his mind free to focus on the important ones. But Nerissa wondered if the real reason weren't simply that he knew he could get away with it.

She finished the last bites of her bread and excused herself from the table. Returning to her room, she paused in front of the mirror and stared at the stranger reflected back at her. All that remained of her beloved, waist-length hair was a close-cropped shag that now clung to her neck and forehead. The front portion was so short it barely reached one-third of the way to her eyebrows. Sunken cheeks and lips from weeks of unconsciousness made her cheekbones and jaw line protrude in an almost masculine way. Green eyes narrowed and watered slightly in disgust and anguish at the virtually unrecognizable image in front of them. Everything else about her appearance was unfamiliar, but at least her eyes were unchanged.

A sudden movement in the reflection made her gasp, and Ildiko's face appeared over the stranger's shoulder.

She squeezed Nerissa's shoulder sympathetically. "Don't despair. Your cheeks will fill out as you recover, and hair always grows back with time," Ildiko said, seeming to read her mind.

"Still, will I ever really be *myself* again? My family, my identity, my country...my future have all been stripped away." Nerissa closed her eyes and turned away from the mirror.

"It is a small comfort, but you aren't the only one to feel this way right now. Think of those men in the kitchen. They failed to perform the most critical of their duties. Our leaders are lost, or were nearly lost, and the country is in our enemy's hands. As a result, their future and the future of our village is in peril. All of their past accomplishments mean nothing in light of this," Ildiko said quietly.

"No!" Nerissa protested. "They are far from failures! Einar saved me. Some gave their lives fighting. What more could they have done?"

Ildiko nodded in agreement. "Yet the Blood and Bond perished. How long will it be until Casimer sends the Senka to find us? They know we have a stronghold somewhere in Chiyo. In hundreds of years, they have never found our village, nor we theirs, but now they are free to move openly within our country."

Nerissa dropped onto the edge of the bed, eyes wide. The security of this village and the safety of the Ohanzee were things she had taken for granted in the weeks since she had awakened. Her expression must have made her thoughts apparent.

"Do not worry about the village. You were unconscious when Einar brought you here, so you didn't see that our location is naturally hidden. The entrance is blocked by a force of nature. There is only one way in and out, and we can bar the path at a moment's notice."

Nerissa couldn't imagine how this was possible, though she had already seen that the village was surrounded by cliffs and mountain tops on all sides. The entrance would be the weak link. No gate or wall was impenetrable. Before she could ask about it though, Ildiko continued on.

"The village wasn't my point. What I'm trying to say is that everyone has done all they can. Circumstances are bad, but nothing can be done about that now. Just don't forget that you are the Blood of Chiyo now—whether you feel like you are or not."

Nerissa's eyes watered again, and she willed herself not to cry. "You reminded me of my mother," she said, brushing at her eyes with one hand. "I'm sorry for being a sullen, angsty mess. All I have now is time to dwell on my misery."

"She was a good woman," Ildiko said in a comforting tone. She rose from the bed. "I think you'll find that Hania's surprise will help you. Remember that Chiyo may be in ashes, but the phoenix will rise again. That is its nature, after all. Now hurry and change. They are waiting for you."

A short time later, Nerissa followed behind Einar and Haku on one of the many cobblestone paths that ran through the village. The dark, rounded stones felt uncomfortably hot beneath her feet, and heat seeped through the thin leather sole of her sandals so readily that she may as well have been barefoot. Even those patches of stones covered in shade were warm. Yet Jin walked beside her, giving no sign that the heat affected him in the slightest.

While Einar and Haku merely nodded and lifted a hand in silent salutation to each person they passed, Jin waved energetically, calling out jovial greetings of good morning. Not wanting to draw attention to herself, Nerissa opted for a simple nod too. Her arrival in the village had already created enough of a stir.

Although a handful of the Ohanzee traveled in and out of the city regularly as part of their duties, strangers entering Darnal were an extreme rarity. According to Hania, it had been twenty years since the last outsiders had come to the city, so it was natural that news of Einar's arrival that night carrying an unconscious young man had spread like wildfire. It was happenstance that had led to the confusion about her identity, but the three chiefs had done nothing to dispel or correct the story.

They encountered fewer and fewer people the closer they got to Hania's home, which was located at the foot of the sheer cliffs lining the far edge of the village. The roar of a nearby waterfall echoed off the surrounding stone walls as they approached. Unlike the other chiefs who could live where they chose, the home of the Chief Advisor was passed from one to the next in succession.

Nerissa assumed that there must be a reason for this, but she had no idea what it was. There was nothing in the outward appearance of the house that seemed different from any others she had seen in the village so far. Perhaps it was related to the smaller, but taller, hexagonal building that was attached to the main house by a covered walkway.

When they arrived, Jin called out to Hania, who happened to be walking between the two buildings. He waved and gestured for them to go ahead and enter the house.

As Nerissa followed the others inside, she scanned the interior for anything out of the ordinary, but there didn't seem to be anything unusual here either. The main room had obviously been decorated with a woman's touch. Ruffled pillows sat on each of the chairs and lace curtains draped the windows. Over the fireplace, was a portrait of a young Hania and a woman Nerissa presumed was Hania's late wife. The only thing she found odd about *it* was that Hania had hair.

"My Lady," Hania said, bowing with a grace most men his age no longer possessed. "Welcome to my home."

Nerissa smiled. "Thank you for the invitation. I hear that you have something to show me? Einar, Haku, and Jin have been quite secretive about what it is."

"The Archives are no secret," Hania said, looking confused.

Einar sniffed and looked away, and Haku folded his arms across his chest.

"We didn't say it was a *secret*," Jin said, laughing. "Just that it would be difficult to describe. I suppose we could at least have told her we were going to the Archives."

"The Archives are easy enough to explain. The next place we will go to..." Einar hesitated, as if searching for the right word. "Well, that place is a bit difficult to describe. And *one* of us still won't be seeing it for some time yet." He directed a pointed look at Jin.

"All of the work and none of the benefits," Jin griped. "You'll tell me about it later won't you, Nerissa?"

She glanced at the three chiefs, unsure how to respond, and the three men shook their heads in unison. "It seems not, Jin," she replied.

Jin feigned a crestfallen sigh and winked. "It was worth a try."

Hania cleared his throat, but the creases at the corners of his eyes belied his stern expression. "The reason why this home is passed from one Chief Advisor to the next is because maintenance of the Archives is one of the role's primary responsibilities. Since you have such a great affection for books, I thought the Archives would be of particular interest to you. You are welcome to spend as much time here as you like, and you may read anything you want. It would be a good way to pass the time while you recover."

"I think that is an excellent suggestion!" Nerissa said. History books were not her favorite reading material, but she suspected these would be considerably more interesting than a textbook.

Hania gestured toward a door on the side of the room. "In that case, come this way."

---

When Nerissa stepped into the Archives, all she could do

was stare at her surroundings. Shafts of sunlight poured down from skylights and filtered through sheer fabrics in a myriad of hues, bathing the room in a rainbow of color. The effect was stunning and reminded her of the stained glass windows of the cathedral in Niamh. She inhaled deeply, basking in the intoxicating aroma of aging ink and paper that permeated the air.

Her pulse quickened with every breath. How many books were here that could not be found in the University Library—even in the Special Collection? What treasures lay hidden in these stacks?

"What do you think?" Hania asked.

"I can't wait to take a closer look!" Nerissa said, rubbing her hands together eagerly. "I have to ask though, who decorated this place? The style isn't particularly…masculine."

Hania chuckled. "Indeed. This is not my work."

"My mother, the previous Chief Advisor did it," Haku added.

Nerissa's eyebrows twitched upward. "So women can be Chief?"

"Of course," Hania said, looking thoroughly perplexed. "Wasn't that obvious?"

Haku, Einar, and Jin all looked equally nonplussed.

"Let me make sure that I understand what you're saying. Women can be rulers. They can be Chiefs. Yet, they are not allowed to be guardians. If women are fit to be leaders, why can't they train and fight side by side with the men?"

Haku folded his arms across his chest again. He was

clearly uncomfortable with the underlying implication of the question. "You seem to have a misperception about the reason why only men serve as guardians."

"It is a very old tradition," Einar said, now looking as uncomfortable as Haku.

Hania wandered away from the group, apparently in search of a book among one of the farthest stacks.

Jin, on the other hand, grinned. "Believe me, if the Ohanzee women even thought they were perceived as being inferior to the men in any way, they would not rest until the idea had been beaten out of us. The tradition has been practiced almost as long as the Ohanzee have existed. It stems from the time of our ancestors, the Gullintanni. At that time, men and women did fight side by side. The leader of the Gullintanni, our founder, was a woman. It was the women who first laid down their swords and swore to never pick them up again. Since that time, no woman among us has taken up the sword."

That revelation caught Nerissa by surprise. "What was the reason?" she asked.

Hania tottered back, having located the book he was looking for. He handed the thick, obviously aged tome to Nerissa. A few bits of leather flaked away in her hands.

"This is the last known copy remaining. Perhaps the Senka have one also. You will find the answer to your question in here. It is a history that dates from King Gared's time. We are uncertain how much of the story is explicitly true and how much is an embellishment. Many stories of Gared's life and accomplishments have become exaggerated over time. Nonetheless, this book is of reasonably good providence. I, and many Chief Advisors before me, consider it to be the most reliable account of his life. It is a better explanation of the origin of the tradition than we could manage to retell here. You'll probably learn quite a few other things that were not in your history lessons as well."

Nerissa ran her hand over the thick book. The cover was embossed with the image of a phoenix and dragon chasing each other's tail. In the center was a thornless rose, the stem of which was clutched by each of the surrounding creatures' claws. Nerissa recognized the symbol as the original crest of Renatus. The title of the book, which was stamped above the crest in now flaking gold leaf, read *The History of the Phoenix, the Dragon, and the Rose*. The author's name had worn away, but Nerissa could make out their title: *Chief Advisor to Gared, the first King of Renatus*.

"The first Chief Advisor," she said, awed. "Hania, I think you are being unnecessarily humble regarding this book's providence."

"No book can tell the whole story of a time," he said. "This is just one volume in the Archives' collection. Others here contain the genealogy of the Royal Family, dating all the way back to Gared. The Records of the Ohanzee describe the history of politics and culture in Chiyo, which is similar to what you have already studied but also includes *our* contributions to events as well."

Nerissa gently hugged the book to her chest. "I can't wait to start reading."

Einar lifted his wrist to check his watch "That will have to wait for now. I have an appointment outside the city later this afternoon, so we need to move on to the next destination."

# 14

## TREASURES

Their next destination turned out to be a nondescript wooden building not far from the Archives. Nestled among a cluster of trees at the foot of the cliffs, the tiny structure was less of a building and more of a hut. Beside the door sat a high-backed chair and a rack holding dozens of small glow lamps.

"I'll wait here," Hania said, settling into the chair.

Jin sighed reluctantly. "Is that my cue to start making the usual rounds?"

"That won't be necessary today," Hania answered. "Stay and keep me company for a while."

As Jin sat down in the grass, Haku pulled a key ring from his pocket and opened the door. Nerissa stepped inside after him, followed by Einar with the rack of glow lamps.

The interior of the hut consisted of a single room, which was unadorned aside from a woven rug on the floor, a few large pillows, and a fireplace on the far wall.

"Is this the mysterious place?" Nerissa asked. "If so, I have to say it is somewhat anti-climactic. And it is definitely not any cooler in here than it is outside."

Haku smirked but said nothing while he locked the entryway door from the inside.

Einar responded by giving her a wry look and then bent over and pulled back the rug to reveal a door in the floor. "Does this make it more interesting?"

Haku unlocked the door in the floor with the second key and lifted the hatch upward. Beneath it was an opening with a ladder leading down into the darkness. They clambered down surrounded by cool, dry air and walked until a stone wall barred them from going any farther.

Upon reaching the dead end, Einar placed two of the glow lamps on hooks that protruded from the walls on either side of the corridor. There was an audible click, and a series of holes appeared in the wall to the left. Einar reached into one of the holes, and the sound of clicking gears echoed throughout the tunnel as he turned some kind of mechanism.

"What is this place?" Nerissa wondered out loud.

"This is the entrance to the vault where the treasury of the Royal Family is stored," Haku answered. "The device on the wall is a type of lock. There are cranks in each of the holes that have to be turned a specific number of times, in the correct order and direction, for the door to open. In addition, it is protected by a mechanism to deter anyone from attempting to guess the combination."

"I've never seen anything like it," Nerissa said. "How

does it work?"

"It will trigger if you make two mistakes. First, a clamp locks down on the intruder's hand while they hold the crank. Then, a blade drops from above the holes in the wall, cutting off their hand. In the process, the blade also severs the cables connected to the door so that it can no longer be used to open the vault."

Nerissa stared at Haku wide eyed and then turned to anxiously watch Einar. He reached into the openings without hesitation, giving no indication that such a violent mechanism lay behind the rock face. After a few more tense moments, a low rumbling began to echo through the chamber, and the stone wall in front of them began to rise.

"Let's go," Einar said once the noise ceased.

But they stopped again on the other side of the opening so that Haku could hang one of the glow lamps onto a hook attached to one of the cables near the ceiling. He nodded to Einar who turned the handle of a crank on the nearby wall.

With a creaking groan, the cable and lamp lurched forward several feet and an empty hook appeared directly overhead. Haku placed the second lamp on it, and Einar turned the crank again. They repeated the process until all ten of the glow lamps hung from the ceiling, spanning the length of the cavern. The lighting was still dim, but it was now sufficient for Nerissa to see what the space held.

The walls were lined with large chests and trunks, some stacked nearly to the ceiling. Scattered among them were smaller containers which had glass doors or tops. Oddly shaped forms draped in dust covers were randomly distributed among the boxes. Nerissa lifted the top of the small box closest to her and saw a sparkling necklace, bracelet, and earrings on a velvet cushion. She remembered seeing her mother wear the set many years ago.

She glanced questioningly at Einar and Haku. "Is this…?"

Haku finished the thought for her. "This is the Royal Family's vault and the personal treasury of the Blood. All of this is yours to do with as you wish."

Nerissa's throat suddenly felt dry. She had always known that her family was very wealthy, and she had some idea of the balance of money kept in her family's account at the bank in Niamh. That amount was already more than any reasonable person would ever need. The savings kept in the National Treasury was enough to run Chiyo for well over a year. Judging by the size and number of chests in this cave, there was easily ten times that much gold here. If she were to move against Casimer, these reserves would be enough to fund the effort.

Now even more curious, she pulled the dusty sheet back from a nearby painting. A woman and a phoenix were posed in the center, wrapped in a swirl of color. The way they were positioned, it was impossible to tell whether the woman was riding on the bird's back or standing with the bird coiling around her. Curls of hair streamed around the woman's face like black flames, interweaving with those of the phoenix, and orange-red feathers of flame mingled with the fabric of her white gown. The woman and the bird were turned toward one another, yet both were focused on a red gem that floated above the woman's outstretched hands.

The painting was beautiful, but something about it made the hairs on the back of Nerissa's neck stand up. She looked down at the nameplate, which was affixed to the center portion of the bottom of the frame. It read in large letters *The Phoenix*. Oddly, there was no artist's name in the empty area below the title.

She let the sheet drop down over the painting again and continued to walk randomly among the boxes, opening the lids of some to peer inside. The wealth accumulated here was incredible, but the amount of history behind the items was even more precious. She let herself wander, stopping here and there to look through containers and pulling back sheets where she felt drawn.

One container, a tiny chest sitting on a stack of other boxes, caught her attention even though there was nothing remarkable about it. Due to its size, it could easily be lost or overlooked in this dim, crowded place. The latch released with a sharp click, making Nerissa worry that it might have broken. The wood was so old that ridges protruded from the surface, and she could feel the pattern of the grain by running her fingers over it.

Inside lay only one item: a cloth pouch. Tufts of fabric flaked off onto Nerissa's hand as she picked it up. Taking care not to break the fragile cord, she opened it and reached inside. The contents were mostly powder with a few small bits mixed in that were sharp like shards of glass. There was a bigger piece too, but she couldn't quite wrap her fingers around it. Did it feel hot to the touch? No, it must have been her imagination.

Intrigued, she poured the contents of the pouch into a small pile on top of a nearby chest. Scattered within the pinkish-red powder were crimson shards. She traced a finger through the dust until she found the largest piece and pulled it out. The deep-red crystal, several inches long, glittered in the lamplight. Cradling the shard in her palm, she blew on it to remove the rest of the powder. As she did so, though Nerissa did not see it, the stone briefly glowed like a hot coal.

Nerissa called out to Einar and Haku who were talking quietly near the entrance. "May I take this with me?"

They both made their way over to where she was standing. Upon seeing the stone in her hand, Einar chuckled.

Haku's brows furrowed. "Of all the treasures here, *this* is what you want?"

"Is that alright?"

"Of course," he replied, still stunned. "We told you before that all of this belongs to you now."

Nerissa coiled her hand around the shard. This would be the first stone to replace her lost collection—and it was a fine piece to start with. She brushed the pile of powder back into the pouch as best she could and then continued meandering among the containers.

Einar and Haku remained where they were. "Of all the treasures here, *that* is what she wanted," Haku repeated. "Antiques, jewelry, art—everything belongs to her, and what is the first thing she takes for herself? A piece of a broken rock."

"I'm not surprised," Einar said. He wore a look of pride on his face. "Once you get to know her better, you'll understand."

# 15

## A PLEASANT AND UNPLEASANT
## SURPRISE

### *Raysel*

The cobblestones were smooth and uncomfortably hot beneath Raysel's bare feet as he made his way through the village. Perhaps he should have worn sandals, but the feeling of being barefoot put a spring in his step after weeks of wearing sweaty shoes for training. His pace was leisurely, as was the pace of those around him. It was too hot to move any faster in the late afternoon heat.

Raysel's mood was lighter than it had been in recent weeks, and not just because today was his first full day off from training. Even his day off wasn't a complete day of rest. His younger sister, Aravind, had once again exhausted her supply of burn cream, so Raysel had volunteered to be the one to fetch a refill from Ildiko.

Humming to himself while tossing and catching the squat little jar in one hand, he gazed up at the sky where puffy clouds drifted lazily by. The ends of the red sash draped around his waist rose and fell in the undulating breeze. He couldn't quite put his finger on it, but it felt like something good was about to happen.

He had nearly reached his destination when he spotted a familiar shadow lurking at the foot of a tree a short distance off the path. His friend's mood was so plain that Raysel could almost see a gray fog hovering around him like a rain cloud. That wasn't really surprising. Rian had a tendency to brood and would often seek out one of his favorite hiding places to be alone. This habit had become particularly frequent since Casimer's attack on Niamh. It wasn't how Raysel chose to handle frustration and regret, yet it *was* Rian's way and had been for as long as Raysel could remember.

Rian didn't acknowledge his approach, so Raysel decided to continue on and made a mental note to stop and talk if he were still there on the way back. He couldn't blame Rian for being upset, considering all that had happened, but his moodiness had lingered for far too long. Raysel himself had felt much the same way at first, although recently his gloom had been tempered by that vague, hopeful sensation.

A short time later, Raysel arrived at the doorstep of Ildiko and Einar's home. He knocked once and then again, louder. When there was no response, he opened the door and poked his head in.

"Ildiko? Hello?" he said, beginning to worry.

*Ildiko has been in comparatively good health lately*, he reminded himself. She was probably busy cleaning or caring for a patient and hadn't heard him. Nonetheless, something could have happened to her while Einar was away, so Raysel let himself in and walked from one room to the next looking for her. There was no sign of anyone inside the house—not even the mysterious young nobleman. Raysel strode through the kitchen and pushed open the door leading into the grassy area behind the house. There, two silhouettes moved among the many lines of laundry hanging out to dry, and Raysel exhaled in relief.

Just as he was about to call out to Ildiko, the wind stirred and lifted the sheet that had been obscuring his view of the nearest figure. Their eyes locked in surprise for a fleeting moment before the sheet descended once again.

Raysel's pulse raced as the jolt of seeing *those* eyes froze him in place. Even though her head was wrapped in a scarf and her cheeks were sunken to an extent that her face was nearly unrecognizable, he had no doubt it was *her*. Those green eyes could only belong to one person. The person he had watched over practically every day for the last three years. The person who he had been born to protect, and the very one he had failed to protect that night.

He had recognized her behind the phoenix mask she had worn at the masquerade, and he recognized her now. Raysel tried to say her name, but his throat was so tight he was unable to make a sound.

"Ildiko, we have another visitor," the figure behind the sheet said.

Though tinged with uncertainty, the sweet familiarity of Nerissa's voice made Raysel's heart soar. It was a voice he thought he would never hear again.

"A visitor? No one else was supposed to come over today." The second silhouette put down their basket, and then Ildiko emerged from the fabric jungle. "Raysel! What brings you here when my home is in such disarray?"

"I think it is safe to say that everyone's home is in disarray when they do laundry, Ildiko," Raysel replied.

"Nevertheless, I'd rather not be the one to confirm that theory," Ildiko said, hastily shooing him back into the house before he could say another word. "I was not expecting company."

Raysel craned his head, trying unsuccessfully to see Nerissa once more. "Ildiko, what is Nerissa doing *here*?"

"Nerissa?" Ildiko looked at him like he had sprouted another head. She pressed one of her palms to his cheek, checking his temperature. "Has the heat taken your mind?"

"Nerissa is helping you with the laundry. I saw her!" Raysel said. He nearly stumbled over his own two feet as Ildiko continued to herd him backward through the house.

"You are mistaken," Ildiko replied flatly.

"No, I'm not. I would know her anywh—" Raysel's heel caught on the front threshold, cutting his protests short and sending him hopping on one foot out the door to avoid losing his balance.

"Then you *are* delusional." Ildiko stopped in the doorway. She raised her chin as she spoke and folded her arms across her waist. "The person out back is a cousin of the late Heiress. He is the closest remaining blood relation to the Royal Family. They bear a familial resemblance and that is all. If you keep insisting you saw the late Heiress, people will begin to think you've gone mad. Am I making myself clear?"

Raysel gritted his teeth. "I understand." The only clear thing was that Ildiko had no intention of admitting the truth or letting him anywhere near Nerissa. He would have to concede for now. "It was quite a shock to see such an uncanny resemblance. I'm sorry to have surprised you. Aravind noticed this morning that she needs a refill of the burn salve. Since no one answered the door, I became worried and let myself in."

Ildiko held out her hand, and Raysel placed the jar in her outstretched palm. "I see. How fortunate for her that the forge is closed today. I've never known anyone even remotely as clumsy as Aravind, but I admire her for not letting it daunt her determination to become a blacksmith," Ildiko said, acting like their previous conversation had never occurred. "Einar will bring the refill over later tonight." And with that, she snapped the door shut, mere inches from Raysel's face.

"Apparently the forge isn't the only thing closed today," he remarked, rubbing his nose protectively and feeling a bit perturbed by the near miss.

# 16

## NOT ONE OF THEM

*Raysel*

Raysel lingered in front of the closed door for a time, clenching and unclenching his fists indecisively, trying to sort through the conflicting thoughts that tumbled through his mind. Knocking again seemed pointless, and he resisted the temptation to force his way in to see Nerissa by climbing the fence at the side of the house. Barging in would frighten her, which was one of the very last things he wanted to do. There was no way that Ildiko could physically prevent him, but doing so would anger her and Einar both.

He exhaled slowly and then turned and walked away from the house. While it was frustrating to wait, the proper way to handle this situation was a direct—and private—confrontation with his father. With the decision made, relief filled the hole that had been in his chest for weeks, and he smiled to himself. Nerissa was alive. She was safe. That was all that mattered for now. As he walked down the path this time, he didn't even notice the heat on the soles of his feet from the stones.

A few minutes later, he returned to the tree where he had last seen Rian. Sure enough, he was sitting in the same place with the hilt of his sword leaning against his shoulder. His eyes were closed, and once Raysel got close enough, he could hear a soft snoring. He could easily pass by without stopping, and Rian would never know. Still, his father wouldn't return for a few more hours, and he really did want to talk to his friend.

He nudged Rian's knees sideways with his foot, knocking Bane's hilt into Rian's cheek in the process. "I know you need plenty of beauty rest, but why waste a rare day off by sleeping the whole time?"

One blue eye popped open, glaring up to see who had dared to interrupt his nap. "It's too hot to do anything else," Rian groused. He yawned and stretched, rubbing his eyes. "You don't look like you're being particularly productive at the moment either."

*If only you knew*, Raysel thought. "As a matter of fact, I'm running an errand," he said instead. "I'm on my way back from dropping off Aravind's jar of burn cream for a refill."

"Ever the dutiful brother," Rian teased while yawning at the same time.

A wry smile crept across Raysel's face. "You could be a dutiful son by helping out your mother and Alala at the school."

Rian grunted. "That just gets me into trouble."

"Oh, that's right. There was some incident where you hit one of the children on the head?"

"Let's be clear. I didn't *hit* him. I bonked him. It was barely a tap, and he deserved it!" Rian argued. He demonstrated by moving one hand up and down in a chopping motion.

"Seriously?" Raysel tilted his chin, incredulous. "What did an eight-year-old do to deserve being 'bonked'?"

"He stole my snack!"

"Hmm…" Raysel wrinkled his nose and thought hard. "I suppose I might have done the same thing in that situation."

"Anyway, those children are scary. I'm not going back. I don't know how Alala and my mom do that every day—and they actually like it."

"Everyone has their calling," Raysel said. "Which reminds me, when are you going to stop sulking and get back to yours?"

"Don't start," Rian warned. "Why does everyone feel the need to lecture me? Even though I'm an outsider and I can't be one of the personal guardians like you, the masquerade assignment was my chance to prove myself *worthy* of being one of the Ohanzee. Is there a problem with me wanting to take responsibility for my shortcomings?"

He huffed, glaring up at Raysel's now expressionless face before finishing. "Obviously, I'm not strong enough or else things would have turned out differently."

"You act like you can do the job of all of the Ohanzee alone. That's an awfully arrogant attitude to have. Although that's not really a surprise since it's *you* we're talking about," Raysel joked. He continued on more seriously. "We all failed that day, myself included."

*All except Einar*, he added silently. "This isn't a one-man show, Rian. I can tell something is bothering you. I thought

182

you would sort it out over time, yet you don't seem any different now than you were weeks ago. So what is it?"

Rian stood and began to pace back and forth with his hand on the hilt of his sword. "I hate it when you do that."

"I know," Raysel said.

Finally, Rian sighed in resignation. "I met a girl at the masquerade. She was already dancing with someone, but I could tell she would rather have been dancing with anyone else. Plus, there was something about her that caught my attention. So I cut in and 'rescued' her."

"Always the hero," Raysel quipped. This was surprising information though. Rian was sulking over a girl? That was new. They both had plenty of attention from girls but were too busy with their own goals to put much effort toward romantic pursuits.

Then something clicked in Raysel's mind. "Wait. Are you talking about the girl I saw you with in the garden?"

"That was her. I really hadn't intended anything initially. Dancing with her was just a way to blend in with the festivities." Rian's voice softened. "She was unlike anyone I've ever met, which sounds foolish because I only spent a short amount of time with her."

He paused and rubbed his forehead. "Don't laugh at me! I know I'm acting like a sappy idiot."

"I'm not laughing. So you met a girl that you were attracted to. A normal person would actually be happy about that," Raysel prodded. Did Rian know that the girl was Nerissa? Somehow he didn't seem to. He *must* not know since romantic relationships between the Royal Family and Ohanzee were strictly forbidden.

Rian's blue eyes flashed. "The last thing I should be worrying about right now is a girl. I don't even know her name, yet I can't make myself stop thinking about her. Whenever my mind wanders, I find myself worrying about whether or not she made it out safely and chastising myself for not going back to check. And don't jump in with a witty remark about how horrible it is for me to be concerned about someone. My job that night was to protect three people. That girl wasn't one of them."

*Oh, but she was*, Raysel thought to himself. If Rian were to find out he had been with Nerissa, it would make his guilt worse for having left her alone in the garden. *That* was a feeling Raysel knew well. It was the very same guilt that had weighed on him until earlier today.

Under different conditions, Raysel would have immediately told his best friend the identity of his mystery woman. These were far from ordinary circumstances, however. One thing Ildiko's reaction *had* made clear was that Nerissa being alive and in Darnal was a carefully guarded secret. He would have to remain tight-lipped for now.

*You'll have to forgive me for not telling you what I know*, Raysel said silently. Then, out loud, he said, "As I mentioned before, you weren't the only one with that duty. I failed too—every one of us did."

"I know," Rian said, pacing faster as he grew more and more agitated. "The problem is that I shouldn't be more concerned with the fate of this girl than I am with the people I was supposed to be protecting. I take my duty very seriously. It has been the focus of my every waking minute for as long as I can remember. Still, every time I close my eyes, I'm haunted by the memory of her in the garden that night."

"I wish I could help," Raysel said sympathetically. That much was the truth. "You should stop brooding over a girl you hardly know. As you said, there are far more important things to worry about right now. She probably doesn't even remember you after everything that happened." It wasn't the kindest thing to say, but, hopefully, it would help Rian to stop ruminating and focus his attention on something else.

Rian turned, Dragon's Bane grinding sharply against its sheath as he drew the blade. He was frustrated and angry, and at times like this, he let his sword do the talking.

"Temper, temper," Raysel said, swatting away the sword now pointed at his chest. There was no need to draw Thorn. "Empty threat, friend. You're going to need to get some new material eventually. You've used that same move since we were kids."

Rian smirked. "You know it's not a threat—it's a challenge. If I need to focus on training, why not start by sparring now? If you don't spend less time talking and more time focusing on your swordsmanship, I'm going to surpass you."

"Is that so?" Raysel taunted. "No. No matter how hard you try, you will never beat me."

"Prove it."

"I'll have to pass. I have errands to run, remember? Let's 'debate' this more tomorrow in training," Raysel said. He waved his hand as he walked away.

There was no doubt in his mind that Ildiko knew he had

seen and recognized Nerissa. She would tell Einar what happened right away. It was rare, but for once it was good to be the Chief Preceptor's son. Tonight, one way or another, he would find out why Nerissa's presence was being kept a secret. The sooner he confronted his father, the better.

# 17

## THE STRANGER IN THE MIRROR

*Nerissa*

Ildiko had not returned by the time Nerissa finished hanging the laundry, so she settled down in a shady patch of grass. Lately, she spent all of her free time mulling over what action to take for the future. There was no doubt in her mind that she needed to take back Chiyo. The difficulty was in how to do it. The books the chiefs had shown her in the Archives this morning would be useful resources, but she couldn't just sit around reading.

Given the opportunity, she would be the first to move against Casimer. There was no way that she would sit back and watch others fight her battles for her. Out of anyone in the world, she had the strongest motive to strike, but her aggression wasn't fueled purely by personal motivations. It was merely a matter of time before the Senka sought out and found Darnal. No matter how well hidden or heavily fortified the city was, no armor was impermeable. The sooner Nerissa took action, the safer Darnal would be.

Leaves rustled in the tree overhead, stirred into motion by a gentle breeze. Though it was a hot breeze, the moving air felt nice. Nerissa closed her eyes and leaned back against the trunk, exhausted from the mild exertion of hanging laundry.

She groaned in annoyance at her achy body. Part of her was so tired and frustrated that she wanted to accept Einar's offer to remain quietly in Darnal and hope the city was never found. The rest of her raged with a silent battle cry that screamed unceasingly to rise against Casimer. It was tempered only by Nerissa's awareness that the situation had to be handled delicately.

If the Ohanzee were to retaliate by assassinating Casimer, the people of Marise were unlikely to willingly accept the change in power. Moreover, the Senka would also have to be dealt with. A direct confrontation with them would lead to bloodshed on both sides and, inevitably, the loss of innocent lives.

Nerissa had to find a way to take back Chiyo without provoking a physical conflict. Right now, Casimer had no idea that she was alive, which was a major advantage. Revealing her presence would cost her the element of surprise, and it would potentially put Darnal in peril even sooner. To complicate matters further, she was both entirely devoid of actual combat skills and in the worst physical condition of her life. She doubted she even had the strength to draw a bowstring.

Here in Darnal, she had access to the best training available, but tradition limited that training to men. Based on what she had learned this morning, if Nerissa wanted to train with them, she would encounter as much resistance from the women as she would from the men.

While she could override the tradition by exercising her authority as the Heiress of Chiyo, one of the first things her mother had taught her was that abuse of power bred resentment in the populace. Still, there had to be a way forward. Nerissa just had no idea what path that may be. The conflicting emotions swirled together, an unrelenting tempest in her mind. Another breeze stirred the leaves above, and Nerissa's thoughts became blissfully fuzzy as she surrendered to sleep.

———————◆———————

Nerissa stood in front of the long mirror in her bedroom, inspecting her costume one last time to assure herself that she would not be recognized upon returning to the masquerade. She pulled free an errant strand of long, curled hair that had become tangled among the orange feathers of her mask and smiled with satisfaction.

Suddenly, the reflection in the mirror rippled, and Nerissa watched, stunned, as her image transformed. The reflection gazing back at her resembled herself, but rather than her orange dress, they wore the same training garb as the Ohanzee men. A black collar embedded with crystals encircled their neck, and a white sword was sheathed at their hip.

Nerissa stared at the familiar stranger, feeling disoriented. That was when she noticed a curious-looking red string wrapped around the stranger's wrist. It glowed with an unnatural light and somehow extended through the mirror unhindered by the glass, spanning the space between them.

Following the cord's path with her eyes, Nerissa was surprised to find the other end of it securely entwined around her own wrist. She stepped forward, reflexively reaching out to touch the mirror. Her fingers met not with the cold touch of glass but instead passed through the surface and interlaced with the warm, outstretched fingers of the reflection mimicking her on the other side.

Nerissa stared nose to nose into a face that was her own, yet wasn't, and asked, "Who are you?"

The reflection tilted their head and grinned impishly. "That's a silly question. I'm you."

---

Nerissa's eyes fluttered open in time to see Ildiko walking toward her carrying two silver mugs. A light film of condensation had formed on the outside, and Nerissa could hear the gentle tinkle of what must be ice inside. Ildiko handed her one and knelt to sit beside her.

"I'm sorry that I was gone for so long," she said.

Nerissa sipped the cold water and sighed happily. "It's alright, especially when you bring back a treat like this! What did our visitor need that kept you for so long? I hope it wasn't an emergency."

"No, it wasn't an emergency. That was Haku's son, Raysel, with a request for a refill of burn salve for his sister. You may recall that she and her mother run the city's forge," Ildiko replied. She cupped her hands around the mug to soak in the coolness.

"Are burns a common occupational hazard for blacksmiths? It seems like their equipment would be sufficient to protect them."

"Aravind is unusually clumsy. She's young though, so I'm sure she'll grow out of it. Until then, she will require a steady supply of salve. Some ingredients for my medicines need to remain cold to preserve them, so they are stored in the ice house. I decided to go there right away. I want to have the salve ready for Einar to take with him when he sees Haku tonight."

The corners of Nerissa's lips quirked up. "You had no ulterior motive, I'm sure." She held her mug by the handle and shook it back and forth to rattle the ice.

Ildiko looked startled momentarily but recovered quickly and winked. "It certainly didn't give me a convenient excuse to follow Raysel to make sure he really left." In a more serious tone, she added, "I don't want anyone infringing on your privacy until you've had ample time to recover and decide what you want to do."

Nerissa gave her a conspiratorial look. "I appreciate both your consideration *and* the ice."

"How are you feeling? You seem more cheerful now than you were earlier."

"Physically, I'm tired, but that's nothing of particular concern. I took a little nap while you were gone and had an interesting dream. It's given me an idea about how to address some of the issues that have been weighing on my mind."

Another hot breeze rustled the leaves around them. Ildiko leaned forward, and the ice cube clinked in her mug. "What idea is that?"

Nerissa recounted her dream and then began describing the idea that it had inspired.

Ildiko's eyes grew wide, and her forehead creased in thought. "That is a bold and unorthodox plan, but I think it may actually be a good way for you to begin moving forward. Still, you should be prepared for resistance because Einar is *definitely* not going to like it."

# 18

## ROSE TEA

*Einar and Tao*

Einar was hot. He was covered in dust. He was sweaty and exhausted. It would be an understatement to say that he was having a bad day. He *should* have enjoyed a rare afternoon off, but instead he'd spent it trekking up and down the mountain to attend an urgent meeting with Erik, one of the Ohanzee informants living outside Darnal.

In the end, the meeting had yielded more questions than information. On the day prior to the attack, Queen Echidna had come to Erik's village and met with a well-known seer named Shae. No one seemed to know exactly what the purpose of Echidna's visit had been. Shae herself had kept completely silent on the topic.

Interestingly enough, just hours before Echidna's visit, Shae had sent Erik to the capital with a message for the Blood and the Bond. She had insisted it was of the utmost importance that the letter be delivered as quickly as possible. Unfortunately, Erik arrived at the Manor after the attack, and the letter was never delivered.

The crumpled envelope was now nestled in Einar's pocket. Once he broke the seal and read the warning inside, Einar understood exactly why Shae had felt the message was urgent. Had her vision been a genuine prophecy? Or did she actually have some previously unknown ties to Marise? Her village *was* near the border between the two countries. Erik believed Shae was loyal to Chiyo but admitted that her behavior had become increasingly peculiar since then.

In Einar's opinion, the whole affair was suspicious. At this point, the most logical course of action was for Erik to continue to monitor Shae's behavior and send word if something changed.

Even though Einar knew having the ill-fated message in hand was important, it still hardly seemed worth the trip. He flipped off his sandals in the entryway with a relieved sigh, wanting nothing more than a refreshing shower.

The prospects for the latter were dashed once he saw both Ildiko and Nerissa waiting for him in the front room. He recognized that look on his wife's face. It was the expression she always had when she was about to say something he wouldn't like. Nerissa's set jaw and the white-knuckled fists in her lap looked equally troubling.

"This isn't quite the scene I had hoped to come home to," Einar said.

Ildiko pressed her lips together until they formed a thin, pale line. "A couple of things happened today that we need to talk about."

"Alright. Which one do you want to start with?" Einar

asked as he dropped onto the sofa with a groan.

Nerissa spoke up first. "I know from dealing with my parents that it is always best to state requests succinctly and assertively, so that's what I'm going to do. I want to become one of the Ohanzee."

"Oh? Well, of course, you are welcome to," Einar responded, feeling relieved. "That was part of the point of taking you to the Archives today."

"No. I think you've misunderstood. I want to learn the ways of combat so that I can fight alongside the rest of the Ohanzee to regain Chiyo." Nerissa's voice was firm, but she twiddled her fingers nervously.

"Absolutely not!" Einar said. Tradition or not, there was no way that he would allow Nerissa to put her life in danger. He could remember, all too vividly, the way he had felt upon finding her bloody and unresponsive in the rubble that night. "I will not let you come to harm again. Aside from the risk associated with confronting Casimer directly, even our training is harsh and the physical demands are—"

"So you want me to be helpless like my parents were?" Nerissa retorted, her eyes flashing.

Ildiko gasped. "Nerissa, that was uncalled for!"

Einar's voice turned oddly calm. "Helpless? I saw my friends die protecting Rica and Parlen. I watched as they were murdered with no way to reach them. I know *exactly* what it is to be helpless, and I wouldn't wish that feeling on anyone! Regardless, only the male Ohanzee train for combat. That is a tradition that has stood since the time of Gared."

"Are you suggesting that you hold a tradition to be of

more value than a command from the Blood of Chiyo?" Nerissa's tone made it sound more like an accusation than a question.

Einar sighed and rubbed his temple, his broad hand obscuring his eyes. "That is not what I am saying at all. You are putting me in a very difficult situation."

"I've already devised a plan that should avoid creating a conflict with your tradition. As much as it pains me to admit it, I should have no problems pretending to be a male if I keep my hair short and bind my chest with a vest worn beneath my clothing. Everyone in the village already thinks that you brought a young nobleman back with you, so we will simply play into that misconception. The disguise presents many advantages. It allows me to train, which will speed my physical recovery. It maintains the element of surprise against Casimer by keeping the fact that I'm alive a secret. And it increases my safety since my alter ego would be viewed as just another member of the Ohanzee—a lower profile target."

"And what do you suggest we call you now? You can hardly go by Nerissa if you're going to pretend to be a nobleman," Einar asked.

Nerissa answered with no hesitation. "Caeneus. You should call me Caeneus."

"I see. From the story of the sea nymph who became a warrior. How appropriate," Einar said, meeting Ildiko's eyes briefly. Judging by the look on his wife's face, the name had been her idea.

He was nearly resigned to the idea when he realized there was a hitch in Nerissa's plan. "There's one problem that you haven't addressed. No matter how well you can alter your appearance, you can't change your voice. There is no mistaking it as anything but feminine."

"I've already considered that, and there is a rather simple solution. I will require you to do a little shopping for me first," Nerissa said with a triumphant smile.

The conversation was interrupted by a knock on the door. Ildiko rose and returned shortly after with Haku's wife, Ebba, beside her. "About the second thing we need to discuss…"

---

Hania, Haku, and Einar sat on the floor pillows in a circle atop the woven rug that concealed the entrance to the Treasury. The small room was stiflingly hot, and the windows would not be opened in order to maintain the privacy of their conversation. A pitcher of ice water sat on the rug between them, a small amenity to make the heat more bearable.

"There are two matters we need to address tonight," Einar said. He dabbed at the sweat on his temple with a cloth. "The first issue is that Nerissa has come to a decision regarding her future here in Darnal."

"What does she plan to do?" Haku asked. "Your expression makes me suspect we may not like what that decision is."

Einar recounted his earlier conversation with Nerissa. On the other side of the circle, Hania sat expressionlessly, staring into his cup as he swirled the ice chunks in slow circles. Haku shifted his jaw, making a conscious effort not to clench his teeth. When Einar finished his explanation, he looked to the other two men. "I'd like to hear your thoughts."

"I see no inherent harm in Nerissa learning to fight and

use the sword. It should help further her physical recovery and improve her ability to defend herself," Hania said without looking up from his cup. "I think having a goal to focus on may lift her spirits as well."

Haku folded his arms across his chest. "I agree with that in principle, but I dislike the idea of breaking with tradition. If her ruse were to be discovered—and sooner or later it *will* be—how will the rest of the Ohanzee feel about our knowingly condoning such a deception?"

Hania shrugged. "It's Nerissa's decision. Our duty to support her plans is greater than any tradition."

Haku sighed and pinched the bridge of his nose. "Duty binds each person differently. While I would do almost anything to uphold my oaths to the throne, not everyone in Darnal would go to the same lengths."

Hania's usually jovial face took on a severe cast, and the contrast was unnerving. "Each person is entitled to their own interpretation of our duty. However, anyone who would work against the will of the Blood of Chiyo is a traitor. It is that simple. My duty is to support Nerissa in every way I can. I will deal with whatever ramifications come my way as a result."

Haku sighed again but nodded in agreement. "I hope it does not come to that."

"I hope so as well," Einar said. "I concur that training is a good idea in principle. The problem I have is that the plan will eventually put Nerissa in harm's way. No matter how hard she works, it will be no substitute for the years of experience and conditioning we all have. Even if she *could* become as strong as the best of the Ohanzee in such a short time, direct involvement in combat would make her vulnerable. I would prefer for us to be the ones engaged in fighting to ensure that she remains safe. And that actually leads me to the second point of tonight's discussion."

Haku leaned back against the wall, arms still folded across his chest. He glanced out the window opposite him just as Ebba passed by while making her rounds. "I suppose the second point is related to my son's discovery this afternoon."

Hania raised an eyebrow. "This is the first I've heard of Raysel making any discoveries."

"Raysel went to Ildiko this afternoon to get a refill of burn cream for Aravind," Haku said. "When no one answered the door, he worried that something may have happened to her, so he let himself in. To make a long story short, he saw Nerissa helping Ildiko hang laundry. Ildiko tried to convince him that the person he saw was not Nerissa, but he knew better."

"I would expect no less of Raysel. I can't imagine that there is a single person in Darnal who doesn't know that being the Heiress' guardian has been his goal since he was a child," Hania said.

"The fact that Raysel knows who she is conflicts with Nerissa's desire to assume a male identity. After all, the more people who know a secret, the more difficult it is to keep," Haku said.

"I don't have any concerns about his ability to keep her true identity a secret," Hania said.

"I gave that some thought on my way here. I have an idea about how we may be able to neatly resolve both issues," Einar said. He waited a moment for the other two to nod before continuing. "Nerissa will not be able to jump into practicing with the others her age. Why don't we assign Raysel to be her trainer as a cover for his *actual* reassignment as her personal guardian? No one would find it odd that he would be the trainer of the person we select as the next Heir."

Hania thrummed his knotted fingers against the damp outside of his cup, deep in thought. "I like this idea," he finally said. "Training together would create a bond of trust between the two of them. They would also be familiar with each other's fighting style, which would make it even easier for Raysel to protect her when they do become involved in a combat situation."

"You make an excellent point," Haku said. "I'm not convinced Nerissa will go through with training once she finds out the intensity required. Still, she would learn the extent of Raysel's abilities and be able to anticipate how he needed her to react. That would make both of them safer in a conflict."

"Then I propose the following: Raysel will be reassigned as her personal guardian and trainer, and we will agree to Nerissa taking on the identity of Caeneus, the next in line to be Heir. Are we in agreement?" Hania said.

Haku and Einar replied in unison. "Agreed."

---

The little gray tea kettle whistled on the stove, but the shrilling sounded muffled to Tao. She was stretched on tip toes as far as she could reach, with nearly her whole torso in the cupboard as she rustled through the cans of tea leaves. She felt restless today, and her mood was currently manifesting itself in the inability to decide what kind of tea she wished to drink. Her hand kept drifting back to the container filled with the rose tea that had been Nerissa's favorite. Tao resigned from her futile search and set the canister back in its place on the shelf. Perhaps she didn't really want tea at all.

She removed the kettle from the stove and gazed out the nearby window wistfully. This late in the evening, few were on the street, and the only sound from outside was the clip-clop of the hooves of an approaching horse and its rider. The clopping stopped as they reached the front of her shop. A moment later, she heard a rapping on the downstairs door, which she ignored at first. The store had closed hours ago. They would just have to return another time.

Another moment passed, and the rapping persisted to a point that Tao could no longer ignore it. She trundled down the stairs and wove her way through the rows of glass cases to the door. The man awaiting her on the other side had a commanding presence. His long reddish-blond hair was laced with silver and pulled away from his face, bound at the base of his neck by a cloth strip. It was a look that had become quite popular in recent years, but this man didn't seem like the type to follow the trends. He did, however, seem familiar.

"I'm sorry, but the shop is closed," Tao said through the door. "Is there something that you need that can't wait until tomorrow?" She did not bother to disguise the small amount of annoyance that crept into her voice.

"I apologize. I realize that it is late in the day, but this is the earliest I could arrive. I'm afraid that I find myself in a rather difficult situation that cannot wait," the man explained.

Tao opened the door and gestured for him to come in. He had been sufficiently apologetic, and his visit really hadn't inconvenienced her that much. Her current mood was hardly his fault. "What do you need that is so urgent?"

"This may seem somewhat trivial, but you know how women are when they get an idea in their head," he began, then hesitated upon seeing the peevish expression on Tao's face. That probably wasn't the right thing to say, he realized. "I understand that you sell a necklace that can lower the tone of someone's voice. I would like to purchase one, if possible."

"You need a voice-changing necklace?" Tao questioned, not really believing that she had heard him correctly. She had told no one about that invention aside from Nerissa. The Heiress would not have told anyone else before Tao officially announced it. If this man knew about the necklace, then *she* must have been the one to send him.

"That's correct," he confirmed.

"It so happens that I have one here. It's the only one I have right now, but this seems to be a special circumstance, so I will give it to you free of charge. Consider it my gift to your lady," Tao said with a wink.

"That isn't necessary. I'm prepared to pay whatever price you require," he replied, reaching instinctively for the pouch around his waist.

"No charge," Tao insisted. "But tell me, you seem familiar. Did you perhaps work at the Manor?"

"At the Royal Manor? You must have me confused with someone else," the man replied smoothly and without hesitation.

"I see. My mistake then," Tao said. She smiled politely as she walked him back to the door. "Please come back again."

"Thank you for your generosity," he said as he climbed

back onto his horse. "I am certain that my lady will be most appreciative."

"I am sure she will be too," Tao murmured to herself, watching him ride away. What was Nerissa up to? Tao supposed that she would find out soon enough.

"I think I might be in the mood for rose tea, after all," she said to the empty shop, now smiling more broadly than she had in weeks.

# 19

## AN OATH IN THE MOONLIGHT

*Nerissa*

The following evening, Nerissa sat at the foot of the falls not far from the Archives. Water tumbled over the cliff from so high above it seemed to touch the crescent-shaped moon before falling from the heights to crash onto an outlying ledge hundreds of feet below. Where the water and the rocky outcropping met, thousands of tiny drops were sent cascading away in a spray that shimmered with the ghost of a rainbow in the moonlight. It was there that the falls divided into twin flows that spilled into the silvery pool in front of Nerissa. The air here held a citrusy fragrance that she couldn't quite identify. The scent seemed out of place but was nonetheless comforting because it reminded her of home.

Nerissa shifted into a more comfortable position, careful to avoid getting the book she'd brought with her wet. She had "borrowed" the tome from the Archives late in the afternoon to escape to the comparatively cooler breezes and shade near the waterfall.

It was growing late now, and the deepening twilight no longer provided sufficient light to read by. Still, Nerissa was content to remain here indefinitely, staring at the moon overhead. The crescent shape it had taken on was her favorite phase. It looked to her like a giant smile grinning down from the heavens. She couldn't linger here much longer though. If she didn't return to Hania's soon, Einar would begin to worry even though she had left a note on the table in the Archives explaining where to find her. She was actually a bit surprised he hadn't come already.

Nerissa idly fingered the crystals on the band that now encircled her neck and wondered if she would really be able to pull off pretending to be Caeneus. She was pleased that the three chiefs had agreed to her plan. Even the stipulation that she have a personal trainer hadn't come as a great shock. A tutor of sorts only seemed logical if she was going to learn as quickly as possible. Einar was supposed to introduce the two of them in the morning.

Nerissa's thoughts were interrupted by a sprig of leaves falling on her head. She pulled the branch from her hair and glanced up in time to see someone drop down from the limbs above.

"Mind a little company?" the young man asked, landing beside her with one hand casually resting on a low-hanging limb. He was dressed in white from head to toe except for the long scarlet belt whose ends swayed from the waist of his loose linen pants. The moon sat just over his shoulder, lighting his snow-white hair from behind like a halo. Once Nerissa recovered from her shock, she realized this was Raysel, the person who had come to see Ildiko for burn cream the previous day.

"I'm afraid I will be poor company, but you're welcome to join me if you like." While she tried to sound indifferent, in truth, she wasn't sure she felt ready to meet any of the villagers yet. Not to mention, she was more than a little bit unnerved that he had approached her without being noticed. Had he snuck up on her? Or had he been sitting in the tree the whole time? The latter didn't seem possible.

Nerissa watched him as he settled in beside her. Even in the dim light, she could see why Ildiko had called Raysel handsome. None of his features were particularly remarkable alone, with the exception of his eyes, but all together they made a striking combination. Those eyes were enough to make Nerissa catch her breath at first glance. They were an intense shade of green, lined with rows of long, dark lashes that tapered to the sharp corners of his eyelids. She felt like his gaze could pierce right through her disguise.

Nerissa shook off the sensation as paranoia. If she wanted to be convincing as Caeneus, she would have to get it together. She inhaled sharply at the realization that the familiar citrusy scent had grown stronger since Raysel had arrived. The scent was coming *from* him, which meant he really had been in the tree the whole time.

Suddenly, she noticed that the brows above the eyes she was gazing into had risen and the rest of his face had taken on a bemused expression.

"Yes?" he asked.

Nerissa blinked, cheeks flushing crimson. "I-I'm sorry," she stammered. "Your eyes are really green."

And there it was—the world's most brilliant recovery. *Men don't stare at one another that way*, she chided herself. No woman with good sense would stare so openly either. She would never pass for a man if she kept up this behavior.

Raysel seemed not to have noticed her squirming, or at least he pretended not to. "My mother calls them viridian," he said. His exaggerated grin brought a wan smile to Nerissa's face.

His expression turned serious as he cocked his head to one side and peered intently into her own eyes. It felt like he was looking through her again, and Nerissa's heart fluttered nervously. "Yours aren't so different from mine. Have you looked in a mirror lately?"

The reflection that greeted her in the mirror every day flashed back into her mind: no curls, no hair pins, no makeup, not even nail polish. Her stylish—feminine—clothes had been destroyed along with her home and replaced by the simple tunic and linen pants favored by the men in Darnal. The awareness of her new appearance made her feel sick to her stomach and painfully insecure.

"As a matter of fact, I have," Nerissa replied curtly, not wanting to dwell on those thoughts. She felt the heat in her cheeks intensify.

Raysel shifted uncomfortably. Clearly she had not reacted to his compliment the way he had expected. He twitched his lips to one side and then the other, as if he were struggling to think of something else to talk about.

"Oh! What was I thinking? I haven't even properly introduced myself. I am Raysel, First Swordsman of the Ohanzee; son of Haku, the Chief Preceptor; and Ebba, the blacksmith." He affectionately patted the sheath of the sword now sitting by his side on the ground. "And this is Thorn."

Nerissa already knew who he was, but Ildiko had neglected to mention that he was the First Swordsman. Unsure what that title meant, she opted for a respectful nod and quickly thought of a way to return the introduction. She hadn't formulated one for her new identity yet, so she chose to keep it short and vague. "I'm Caeneus, formerly of Niamh and currently residing with Ildiko and Chief Einar."

Raysel's face took on an unreadable look, and then turned to stare silently at the waterfall. They sat awkwardly without speaking for several minutes. The only sound aside from the distant roar of the waterfall was the creaking of Raysel's sandals as he wiggled his toes.

"Since I'm new to Darnal and the Ohanzee, I hope you won't mind me asking this. What does it mean that you are First Swordsman?" Nerissa asked, attempting to break the uncomfortable silence.

"It means that I am considered the highest-ranked swordsman among all the Ohanzee." It was an impressive title, but Raysel's voice sounded wistful instead of proud.

"That is quite an accomplishment, considering the skill of your peers. You don't sound honored by it though." Nerissa hoped he wouldn't be insulted by the observation.

Raysel chuckled mirthlessly. "A title by itself has no value. It is what you accomplish that is important, and I don't feel particularly worthy of it these days. I am glad to have the chance to redeem myself now."

Nerissa could definitely empathize with his feelings. "It seems that we share similar sentiments."

"In what way?"

"I find myself in a village that I've never heard of, surrounded by strangers, and possessing a claim to a royal title for a country that has been seized by a foreign king," Nerissa replied. "I don't feel worthy of all the faith the Ohanzee have put in me, but I will do my best to take back the throne and *become* worthy."

"I will do everything I can to help you take back your title," Raysel said.

Their eyes met again. Raysel's were narrowed with determination while Nerissa's were confused from the implication that came with his declaration to help her take *back* her title.

"For what it's worth, I think you're far too pretty to actually pass for a boy," Raysel said as if trying to answer her unspoken question.

"Are you saying I look like a girl? That's rather rude!" Nerissa tilted her chin up in feigned indignance and hurriedly looked away. She hoped she made it sound like that had been the most absurd comment ever, even though she was secretly pleased by the compliment. It would have been much more convincing had the last words not sounded choked.

"You don't need to keep up that story with me. I knew who you were the moment I saw you peeking out from behind the laundry." He leaned in close, his breath warm on her ear as he whispered, "Nerissa."

Nerissa gasped and involuntarily jerked away from him, her startled eyes wide. Her heart fluttered again, and she was unsure whether it was caused by hearing her real name or from the tingling sensation his whisper had triggered on her ear. Alarm flooded her falsely deepened voice. "How did you know? I hardly even recognize myself!"

"I've watched over you almost every day for the last three years. I would know you anywhere, in any disguise," Raysel said. Nerissa's cheeks turned bright red again. When she said nothing, he rushed on with his explanation. "In addition to being the First Swordsman, I was your personal guardian. That is a title I lost on the day you supposedly died. And it is a title I was given back after I discovered you were still alive."

"I was told my parents had personal guardians, but no one said I had one too."

"I was assigned to be your guardian when you were officially named Heiress. I watched over you part of the time, and Einar watched over you the rest of the time. Normally, you and I wouldn't have met until you took the oath as the Blood of Chiyo, at which point I would have become your guardian full time. But recent events have altered those traditions."

"I can't believe that I had no idea someone was watching me all the time. I do recognize the scent of your cologne though. I was thinking earlier that it reminded me of home. Wearing cologne isn't exactly discreet for someone who is supposed to be in hiding."

"I suppose I wanted to somehow let you know I was there, even if I couldn't tell you." Raysel's cheeks flushed slightly.

"Why didn't anyone tell me about you before?"

"I'm not sure. I expect that they planned to explain everything to you once they introduced us."

"I guess that makes sense." Nerissa twirled the sprig of

leaves between her thumb and forefinger thoughtfully. "Were you at the masquerade that night?" she asked after a brief pause. If he had been there, perhaps he could help fill in some of her lost memories from that day.

"I was, but not for long. Einar was on duty watching over you and your parents at the party. I was coordinating patrols of the festivities around the Manor itself. When suspicious activity was reported at the docks, I went inside only long enough to gather reinforcements."

"I see," Nerissa said, disappointed.

"I did see you in the garden right before the attack. Every day since then, I have regretted telling you to go back inside. I should have escorted you directly to Einar or stayed there to protect you myself. Instead, I followed protocol, thinking Einar knew where you were. I didn't know you had changed costumes or that Einar thought you were in your room. One of our men died guarding an empty room."

Nerissa's heart dropped into her stomach. A man had died in vain, all because of her selfish wish to enjoy the festivities anonymously that night. "If I had…"

Raysel cut her off sharply. "I didn't mean to imply that you were at fault. If you had been in your room, you would have died that night, too, and all would have been lost. Instead, you are here, safe. Regardless of how it came to be, that is all that matters."

Nerissa still looked shaken. Raysel reached to take her hand to comfort her but withdrew, uncertain if she would consider the gesture to be too familiar. He may have watched over her for years, but, from her perspective, they were strangers meeting for the first time.

"Let's not dwell on the past," he said. "What matters now are your plans for the future. Einar asked me to come over tomorrow to make introductions, but since you showed up underneath my favorite 'hang out,' I didn't see any reason to wait."

"So you really were sitting in the tree this whole time?" Nerissa asked, incredulous.

"Yes, although to be fair, I didn't notice you were here until I woke up a little while ago."

One corner of Nerissa's lips twitched upward. "Do you make a habit of sleeping in trees?"

Raysel's laugh brought a full smile to Nerissa's face. "Actually, I do—particularly following a hard day of training in the middle of the summer. If you sleep under the tree, eventually the shade moves, and you end up in the sun. Up in the branches, it stays shady all the time, so it makes far more sense to sleep *in* the tree."

"When you put it that way, it doesn't sound strange," Nerissa replied with a small laugh of her own. "I guess I'll have to make a habit of checking the trees before I sit down so I don't disturb anyone's nap."

"You can, but from now on that will be my job."

Nerissa remembered his earlier comment about visiting the next day so that Einar could make introductions. "Am I correct in assuming you are the one who has been assigned as my trainer?"

"Yes, from now on I will be both your trainer *and* your personal guardian." His eyes locked onto hers once more, his expression serious. "I swear I will not allow you to come to harm again. I will protect you even if it means dying myself."

Nerissa looked down, ashamed of and uncomfortable with the idea of anyone else being killed or injured for her sake. When she looked up again, her eyes flashed with resolve. "I will work as hard as I can to learn to protect myself so that neither you nor anyone else will ever need to sacrifice yourselves for my safety."

"Well, dying to protect you would be a last resort," Raysel replied, his tone oddly light. "I can only be certain I've kept my promise to you if I'm alive to see it for myself. Would you feel better if we both promise to work our hardest to protect each other?"

He held out his hand, pinky finger extended toward her in a gesture Nerissa hadn't seen in years.

Her expression eased, and she curled her pinky around his. "It's a promise." They shook three times, but Nerissa held tight a little bit longer before drawing back. She could still feel the warmth where their skin had met. "Since it seems we'll be spending a lot of time together, why don't you tell me more about yourself? All I know is who your parents are, that you are First Swordsman, and that you have a penchant for silently communicating your presence through cologne." Nerissa counted off each of the facts on her fingers as she listed them.

Raysel quickly turned away, but Nerissa could see that the tips of his ears had turned bright pink. She smirked inwardly. He had seemed so composed this whole time that it was nice to think that, perhaps, she had made him as flustered as he made her.

Raysel leaned back against the tree and sighed, his sandals creaking as he wriggled his toes. "Really? We finally meet and *that* is your first impression of me? Rian would have a good laugh at the irony. I have trained for as long as I can remember with the sole intention of one day becoming your guardian. I am the youngest ever to be named First Swordsman *and* the youngest to serve as personal guardian."

"I-I-I wasn't aware of all of that," Nerissa stuttered.

"It's alright," Raysel said. His expression was a mixture of damaged vanity and demure pride.

Nerissa's jaw dropped. His feelings weren't hurt—he was toying with her! Well, she wasn't going to fall for that any longer. "Aren't you awfully one-dimensional? Does someone so young and accomplished have no time outside of training for hobbies?"

Raysel tilted his head and gave her a sideways smirk. "It so happens that I traveled throughout Chiyo as part of my training and used the opportunity to amass a significant crystal collection."

Nerissa's ears perked up. "Ildiko did say that you had a collection."

"I've been interested in crystals for a long time. According to stories passed down in my family, one of my great-grandfathers, many, many greats ago, was in an incident involving a crystal that turned his hair white. As a result, all of the males in our family have white hair." He flicked the end of his long ponytail over his shoulder. "I don't know if it is true or not, but I've been interested in the potential powers of crystals ever since."

"I think it could be true. Heredity in plants works in a similar way. The color of the flowers or shape of the leaves is

214

passed from one parent to the daughter plants. I'm sure it must work the same way in humans."

Raysel snorted. "Are you comparing me to a plant?"

"N-n-yes," Nerissa admitted, stammering momentarily. "I'm sorry. I didn't mean it as an insult. I studied horticulture at the university…"

Raysel's laughter interrupted her faltering explanation. "I'm named after a plant, but I've never actually been regarded as one before."

Nerissa giggled despite herself.

"What's so funny over here?" Einar's deep voice interrupted.

"Just making conversation with this book thief I found loitering under my tree," Raysel teased.

Nerissa bit her lip and feigned a glare at Raysel. "I was minding my own business reading when this tree-dweller dropped in on me."

"I see," Einar drawled. "Should I assume there's no need for formal introductions tomorrow?"

"I think we covered the important bits already, but I will still come by tomorrow as planned," Raysel said seriously. He stood and offered a hand to help Nerissa up. "Until then."

"Until then," she echoed, handing Einar the book she had taken from the Archives.

Einar shook his head. Did anyone follow protocol anymore?

# 20

## THE OTHER STUDENT

*Nerissa*

The summer passed by in a blaze of heat and sunlight. Nerissa spent her mornings conditioning with the juniors group and her evenings learning basic sword forms from Raysel. Once Ildiko had deemed her fully recovered from her injuries, she resumed archery training with Einar twice a week as well. Afternoon rest time, in the heat of the day, was either spent in the Archives reading, relaxing with Raysel at his family's home, or—her favorite combination—reading at the Archives with Raysel.

On this particular afternoon, Nerissa arrived on the doorstep of Raysel's family home a little earlier than usual. Every time she visited, she couldn't help but admire the exterior of the house. It was covered in endless tumbles of flowers that were so dense they appeared to seamlessly spill forth from every window box in fragrant clusters, creeping up the walls in a mix of thorns and petals. It was obvious that Raysel's mother was as passionate about flowers as she was about being a blacksmith.

Nerissa tapped the iron knocker on the door and hoped it could be heard over the repetitive clang of metal resonating from the smithy next door. When there came a response that sounded vaguely like "come in," she opened the door and stepped directly into the large common room that served as both the living area and kitchen. Here, there were only slightly fewer flowers than outside. Garlands of dried blossoms draped in swags along the trim of the high ceilings and lined the tops of door frames. Elaborate wreaths decorated the walls, and dried herbs hung in carefully tied bundles from the fireplace hearth. The room also lacked no shortage of fresh flowers, undoubtedly cut from the gardens surrounding the house. With the windows open, the interior was a fragrant cloud.

Nerissa noticed two strange things right away. First, Raysel's older sister, Cattleya, was oddly absent from her workstation in one corner of the room. While Cattleya had not exactly taken up her mother's trade, she still followed in her footsteps by choosing to work with gold and silver as a jewelry designer.

No one in Raysel's family did anything by halves, and Cattleya was no exception. Her jewelry was both beautifully distinctive and of remarkable quality. Her creations were taken into Niamh to be sold by Ohanzee contacts—as were many of the products created by artisans in Darnal.

Nerissa had been surprised to discover that she'd unknowingly owned several of Cattleya's pieces, although those were all lost on that terrible night along with everything else. This was the first time that Cattleya had not been hard at work when Nerissa came to visit, and she couldn't help but wonder where the older girl was.

The second strange sight was a pile of laundry with legs,

teetering its way through the room. It moved precariously along a course leading away from the back door and heading roughly toward Raysel's bedroom.

"Would you like a hand with that?" Nerissa asked.

"No, I've got it," the laundry pile replied though it sounded more like, "Mo, mphhmogit."

Shaking her head at his stubbornness, Nerissa crossed the room and opened Raysel's bedroom door.

"Fffanx," said the laundry.

Nerissa smirked and followed the pile as it tottered into the room, picking up the random clothing dotting the floor behind it like a breadcrumb trail. Somehow it made it across the room without banging its shins on any furniture and dropped into a heap on the bed, revealing Raysel beneath. Nerissa tossed the pieces she had collected in with the rest.

"You couldn't have used a basket?" Nerissa asked.

Raysel gave her a wry look. "Cattleya had both of them filled with her laundry already."

"Where is she today? It's odd for her not to be here," Nerissa mused. She wandered around the room, idly fussing with random crystals from Raysel's collection as she came across them while he folded clothes.

"She went out with my grandmother to the market. *Again.*"

Nerissa's brow's furrowed. "That's the third time this week."

"They forgot to buy peppers for tonight's dinner," Raysel said, sounding vexed. "No doubt their sudden bout of forgetfulness is directly related to the fact that Cattleya has taken a liking to the shopkeeper's son. Never before have I eaten so many peppers, beets, and radishes."

Nerissa laughed. "Has he taken a liking to her as well?"

"I don't know. I'm not sure if I want him to or not."

Nerissa couldn't stop herself from laughing again. Raysel protectiveness of his sisters was both sweet and unnecessary. "It seems your grandmother approves, at least."

He shrugged noncommittally and began folding another pair of pants. "How was conditioning this morning?"

Nerissa flopped into the one chair in the room and let her head roll to the side listlessly. "It was exhausting, as always. No matter what shape I'm in, I will never enjoy running long distances."

Raysel nodded in commiseration and continued folding quietly, anticipating that Nerissa wasn't finished yet.

"I can say that I no longer have trouble keeping up with the rest of the group. I suppose that's something to be happy about."

"You've come a long way in a short period of time," Raysel replied. "You won the summer archery competition. You beat out the very best archers of the Ohanzee. Rian held that title for three years in a row, so taking it from him is a huge accomplishment!

"You should have heard Einar bragging about how his two best students placed first and second. Not only have you recovered from your injuries, but you've also improved your condition to be on a level with many of those who have been training for years."

Nerissa sighed in exasperation. "I can still do better."

"Overachiever," he teased.

Nerissa rolled her eyes. "Isn't that like the pot calling the kettle black?"

"I guess it is," Raysel admitted. He laid the last folded item down on the pile and crossed the room to pick up a small pouch from the top of his dresser. "Consider this a congratulatory gift for winning the archery competition," he said as he handed Nerissa the pouch.

"You didn't have to get me anything," she replied, but she didn't hesitate to open it and pour the contents into her free hand.

In her palm was a black leather cord and the red fire-fire crystal she had taken from the Treasury. The crystal was now wrapped in a filigree coil of gold so that it could be worn as a pendant.

"So *this* is why you wanted to borrow the stone from me," she exclaimed. She held the cord in front of her so the pendant spun in the light from the nearby window. "It's beautiful! Did Cattleya make this?"

"I admit that I did have an ulterior motive when I asked to borrow it. Cattleya finished it yesterday, and I couldn't wait any longer to give it to you."

Nerissa noticed the tips of Raysel's ears had turned slightly pink. She blinked to ease the burning sensation building at the corners of her eyes.

"Thank you," she said. The words were nowhere near sufficient to express her gratitude. This was the only thing that really belonged to her now. It had been so long since she had worn a piece of jewelry, aside from the voice-altering choker, that her chest ached with happiness to be able to wear this necklace . As silly as it seemed, it was as if he had given her back a little piece of her old self.

"You're welcome, of course," Raysel said. He tugged at the leather strand around his neck to pull free his own pendant—a rare type called a "phantom" crystal. Phantom crystals were those that contained another, smaller one within it. Raysel's was clear with a green phantom inside. "The leather cord is like mine, so it is durable enough for you to wear it during training. Just tuck it underneath your shirt beforehand."

"Can you help me put it on to get the length right?" she asked, standing up from the chair.

Raysel dropped his own pendant back down inside his shirt and reached out to take the one Nerissa held. When he touched it, Nerissa saw the stone emit a brief flash of red light.

"Did you see that?" she exclaimed.

"See what?" Raysel asked, confused.

"That red flash! The crystal glowed when you touched it."

"Really?" Raysel held the crystal closer to his face, examining it with interest. "I don't see anything now. It feels warm, but that's probably because you were holding it. Are you sure it didn't happen to catch the light?"

Nerissa frowned. She was almost certain the crystal had been shadowed by his hand. Still, it wasn't impossible for it to have been struck by light from the window. "I guess that must have been what happened," she relented. What other explanation could there be? Even when crystals were being used, they didn't change in appearance.

Raysel handed the pendant back to her. "Well, since you're wearing it now, you'll know if it happens again."

"That's true," Nerissa said. She held it at the appropriate length and passed the ends of the leather cord over her shoulder.

Raysel tied the ends and Nerissa let go of the pendant, allowing it to hang freely. She wanted to admire it for a while before tucking it away for evening practice.

"Ready for lunch?" Raysel asked, already heading for the door.

"I'm starving," Nerissa groaned. She followed him out and into the kitchen, twiddling with the pendant as she walked.

◆

Late that afternoon, Nerissa and Raysel arrived at the main practice area in the center of the village. The juniors group she conditioned with met in a separate outdoor area, so this was her first time visiting the building. The exterior resembled a very large barn. And, like a barn, the floor was covered with copious amounts of hay. That, however, was where the similarities ended.

As they made their way through, Nerissa could see that the vast interior was divided into four sections of varying sizes. Nearest the entrance was a warm-up and rest area with jugs of water. The second area was filled with numerous wooden and hay-stuffed training dummies, which were arranged in assorted heights and positions. Several of the Ohanzee were there sparring independently, using practice swords made of tightly wrapped bundles of wood strips.

In the third section, targets hung from ropes tied to the

overhead beams in a roughly circular arrangement. One man, tall and broad-shouldered, stood in the center of the circle, fending off targets that were randomly swung at him by his cohorts. Nerissa's eyes widened at the realization that he was practicing with a real sword.

Two targets descended toward him almost simultaneously, one from the front and one from behind. Nerissa winced in anticipation of the impact, but it never came. In one continuous motion, the man lunged forward with his sword, slicing smoothly through the first target, and then spun to deflect the one behind.

"Impressive," Nerissa breathed. She was startled to hear a chuckle beside her.

"Should I be jealous?" Raysel asked.

"Jealous?" she replied, confused.

"You've never said that about *my* skills."

Nerissa scoffed. "I think as First Swordsman, your skill level is well established. Besides, the only time I see yours is when we are practicing. At that point, I'm too focused on defending myself to admire much of anything."

"I suppose," Raysel said in mock disappointment. "His name is Jarold. He practices both swordsmanship and hand-to-hand combat. To be honest, if he had chosen one specialty to focus on, he probably would be a better swordsman than I am." Raysel looked over at the sparring ring. "We should hurry or we'll miss the first match."

Nerissa gave Jarold's practice a parting glance and then continued on with Raysel. As they approached the sparring ring, the fourth and largest area, she could see that the first pair had already started. The ring consisted of a circular, roped-off area about five meters in diameter. Around the outside were benches for observers and those awaiting their turns.

Everyone was dressed in the same style tunics and loose fitting pants, but Raysel and the instructor were the sole ones wearing white. That color was reserved for those who have reached the level of a master swordsman.

Though they could wear their hair in any manner they chose during free time, all of the men now had their hair pulled into ponytails for practice. It was an Ohanzee tradition that skill level be indicated by how high the ponytail was worn. The closer it was to the crown, the higher the individual's rank.

While Raysel and the group's instructor were the only ones wearing theirs at the crown, this was an advanced group so all of the men present wore theirs high on their head. Seeing them made Nerissa acutely aware of her own hair, now pulled into a stumpy ponytail at the base of her neck. She supposed she should just be grateful that it had finally grown out enough to be able to tie it back.

She took a seat beside Raysel on one of the open benches as the clack and crack of wooden sword on wooden sword filled the area. When the next pair entered the ring, Raysel leaned over so Nerissa would be able to hear him over the clatter.

"The rules are pretty basic. The opponents walk to the middle of the ring and shake hands. Then, they take up their starting position on one of those two lines." He gestured toward the two chalk lines drawn a meter or so apart in the center of the ring. "After the instructor counts down, the match begins. It will continue until one opponent steps out of the ropes or the instructor says 'finish.' It is important to keep going until then. Sometimes the instructor will allow the match to continue even if someone is down or injured. It gives an opportunity to practice escaping from a situation that could be fatal in a real fight."

"I understand," Nerissa replied.

Raysel pointed toward the shorter of the two men in the ring. "Leal is about your height. See how he uses the height difference to make himself a smaller target? If you position your body correctly, similar to his technique, you can significantly reduce any openings you may leave due to your inexperience. Leal is near the master level, so he is a good role model for you."

Nerissa nodded and watched Leal's movements intently. As the practice moved on, Raysel continued to call attention to the strengths and weaknesses of each of the men's techniques and to suggest ways Nerissa could incorporate those suited to her.

The second to last match finished, and the instructor called for the final pair. The first opponent, a tall, olive-skinned man near Nerissa and Raysel's age, entered the ring. His long black ponytail swished side to side as he strode to the center.

Even though they had never been formally introduced, Nerissa recognized him as Raysel's friend, Rian. Raysel had once told her that Rian, his mother, and his aunt were the only outsiders to enter Darnal in decades, aside from Nerissa herself. He was the one she had defeated in the finals to win the archery tournament. Having watched his earlier matches, Nerissa could tell he was an accomplished swordsman in addition to being the former archery champion.

Rian assumed his position in the center of the ring, and the instructor called his opponent's name once more.

"My arm is too injured to go again," the man said from his seat on the adjacent bench. He cradled his elbow, which was already swollen and showing a red and purple bruise.

"Understood. Make sure you take care of that," the instructor replied. He turned to Raysel. "What about having Caeneus step in?"

Raysel turned to Nerissa. "It wouldn't hurt to get experience against someone other than me. Don't worry about trying to win, focus on holding him off for as long as you can."

"Alright," Nerissa agreed, despite feeling apprehensive about jumping into a pairing where she was clearly outmatched.

"Don't worry. Rian will go easy on you. He knows you're a beginner," Raysel said, clapping her shoulder encouragingly.

Nerissa picked up one of the practice swords and walked into the ring. The two shook hands, and she noticed Rian's hand was firm and strong, lacking the heavy calluses many of the other trainees had. She also noticed that he squeezed a bit too hard. Had that been on purpose?

"Let's see if you have learned to use the sword as quickly as you learned the bow!" he hissed through clenched teeth while the instructor counted down.

Hesitating, Nerissa stepped back right as the instructor called out "begin." "I-I- didn't just start...," she stammered. The first thrust of Rian's sword cut her off before she could finish saying "learning the bow." She barely managed to block the thrust but quickly regained her footing.

Raysel jumped up from the bench and hovered at the edge of the ropes, ready to jump in if necessary.

Nerissa managed to block each of Rian's advances by staying low like Leal had done in the first match they had watched. She knew she was leaving her midsection open, but it was all she could do to meet his sword blow by blow.

It seemed Rian noticed this too. It was not long until he managed to deliver a solid hit directly to her abdomen. Nerissa gasped and stumbled backward, clutching her stomach as she dropped to the ground.

"Looks like you have a lot of work to do," Rian taunted as he walked away.

"It is not necessary to be so hard on a novice," the instructor reprimanded. "Or perhaps Caeneus is already so accomplished that all of your strength was required?" His sarcasm was readily apparent.

Before Rian could respond, Nerissa swung her leg and swept his feet out from under him. He landed with a thud and then spun onto his side, scrabbling instinctively for his practice sword.

Nerissa rose from one knee, still gulping for air. "The match isn't...over...until the instructor says...'finished,' " she panted, staring down at him fiercely. "Even a novice like me knows *that* much."

"This match is finished," the instructor said immediately. In his haste to chastise Rian, he had indeed forgotten to declare the end.

Rian stared up at those eyes, stunned. His mouth moved wordlessly. Suddenly, Raysel was between them. Two pairs of green eyes glared down at Rian—the furious eyes of his best friend and the eyes that had haunted him since the night of the disastrous masquerade.

# 21

## CREEPING AND CRAWLING

*Rian*

It was late evening by the time Rian approached the clearing behind Raysel's family home. The sun had already dropped below the horizon, and the fiery glow of the last rays of light would soon fade into dusk. Rian's curiosity was piqued so greatly that he was no longer irritated by the fact that Caeneus had taken him down with a cheap shot at the end of their match. The fact that Caeneus was somehow connected to the girl from the masquerade overrode his anger. There was no way he was mistaken—the memory of those same eyes gazing back at him from behind that feathered mask and the image of her standing in the glow of sunset in the garden at the Manor were burned indelibly into his mind.

After the group's sparring practice, he had overheard Caeneus telling Raysel he was feeling well enough to carry on with their usual private lessons. Rian had waited to follow the pair until he was confident they would be too preoccupied to pay attention to their surroundings in much detail.

Rian parted the tangle of branches in front of him and stepped silently into the undergrowth that bordered the far edge of the clearing. The distinctive rapping of practice swords could be heard, but he couldn't see either Caeneus or Raysel yet.

It was too dense to move forward on foot, so he dropped to his hands and knees and slowly crawled forward. He immediately regretted not having returned home first for bug repellant oils or at least a long-sleeved shirt. It was just his luck that all manner of mosquitos and biting insects in Darnal had chosen to inhabit this particular shrub tonight. Well, a few bug bites would be a small price to pay for the information he wanted.

Ohanzee tradition prohibited women from taking part in combat, so it didn't make sense that Caeneus and the girl could be one and the same. But if they weren't the same person, what other explanation could there be? Perhaps they were siblings? Caeneus' voice had been unmistakably masculine, after all. He supposed it was possible that siblings could share such similar features.

If they were siblings, that would be bad news. The chiefs had told everyone that Caeneus was a distant relation to the Royal Family whose own family had also perished in the attack. So if the two really were siblings, then that would mean the girl had not survived that night.

Rian gritted his teeth and kept crawling. He couldn't accept that possibility. If Caeneus were the girl from the masquerade, she was either hiding her identity from Einar and the other two chiefs or they *did* know and it was being kept a secret from everyone else. The latter seemed the most logical. Still, why would her real identity be kept secret, and who else was in on it?

Finally reaching a point where he could observe the pair without being spotted, Rian carefully maneuvered into a sitting position. One of the last cicadas of summer chirred shrilly nearby, but he could hear Raysel and Caeneus well enough. He folded his arms across his chest tightly and watched the pair sparring in front of him.

Rian knew how protective Raysel was of his sisters. He was far too chivalrous to harm a woman—even if it were for training. Based on how he behaved during practice, Rian should be able to determine whether or not Raysel was in on the secret.

Rian slapped a mosquito on his arm reflexively and then froze, hoping the sound hadn't called attention to his hiding spot. Neither Caeneus nor Raysel seemed to have noticed, so he exhaled a long, relieved breath. Another bug buzzed by his ear and he flinched, flapping the air to shoo it away. The pair in the clearing continued to spar uninterrupted, unaware of the entomological war being waged on their audience.

Rian noted that Raysel held the sword in his left hand, rather than the right. He was holding back by not using his dominant hand, but doing so wasn't unusual for an instructor with their student. It tempered the difference in skill levels to a degree and provided good practice for the instructor as well. Being able to wield the sword with both hands was an essential skill, particularly in the event of a debilitating injury to the dominant one. Even with his left, Raysel was still better than many of the other Ohanzee members at their best.

Raysel suddenly jabbed toward Caeneus' left shoulder and was just barely blocked. He quickly side-stepped and swung again, this time at Caeneus' sword arm. The blow connected with a resounding crack. Rian winced at the same time that Caeneus groaned and dropped his sword.

"Are you alright?" Raysel asked.

Caeneus nodded yes, even though his face was contorted in a grimace.

"Let us continue," Raysel replied indifferently.

Caeneus stooped over to pick up the dropped sword and moved into position. Raysel readied himself as well. He counted down and the sparring began again.

Caeneus' movements were much slower now, and Raysel was relentless. He struck at Caeneus' opposite shoulder and was blocked, then sidestepped, swinging at the sword arm. Caeneus tried to dodge away from the blow but wasn't quick enough. When the sword landed with a crack once more, Caeneus cried out in pain and dropped to the ground.

This time Raysel didn't ask if Caeneus was alright. He returned to the starting position and waited for Caeneus to rise. To Rian's surprise, Caeneus only lingered a moment before standing and readying himself.

Rian lashed out at yet another bug as it landed on his forearm, careful to brush it away rather than slapping it. Male or female, Caeneus was definitely tougher than he had initially given him credit for.

In the clearing, the pair started over. Caeneus' reactions were even slower than they had been earlier. It was not long until Raysel drove for the shoulder again. Caeneus managed to deflect the blow with a glancing shot from his own sword and tried to dodge. This time he threw up his left hand to block the anticipated strike to his sword arm. Raysel landed the blow anyway, connecting first with Caeneus' open palm and then once more to the upper arm. Caeneus dropped to his knees, and Raysel returned to the ready position, waiting.

That was enough for Rian. He got back onto hands and knees and carefully crawled out the way he had come. Though it appeared to be cruel on the surface, Raysel's behavior wasn't really. It was the same method that any Ohanzee instructor would have used. It was a highly effective way to learn, but also very painful.

After everything he had seen, Rian knew one thing for sure. There was no way that Raysel would use that method of teaching if he knew that Caeneus was a girl. Caeneus was either the brother of the girl from the masquerade or her identity was being kept a secret from Raysel too.

# 22

## FULL MOON

*Nerissa*

When Raysel finally called an end to sparring practice, Nerissa dropped to the ground and sprawled on her back, staring up at the darkening sky. "That's probably about the same color that my arm is going to be tomorrow," she said wryly.

"I'm sorry," Raysel said. He reached inside his bag of supplies and pulled out a canteen of water for each of them. "I told you when we began training that I wouldn't treat you differently than I would anyone else in the Ohanzee."

Nerissa sat up, wincing as she moved her arm. "I wouldn't want it any other way, Raysel. I knew training would be difficult from the beginning."

"If I were to go easy on you, it could end up costing one or both of us our lives someday. That being said, if I have to cause you injury, then you will at least allow me to patch you up afterward." He reached into the bag again and withdrew a bundle of cotton gauze and various salves.

One corner of Nerissa's lips quirked upward. "You tell me that after every practice," she said. "One day I will be good enough that you won't have to patch me up."

She pulled the light outer tunic over her head with a groan, revealing the sleeveless top she always wore beneath. Wearing two layers made it easier for Raysel to treat her injuries. It made him feel better to attend to her wounds himself, and from Nerissa's perspective, it saved them from having to go back to Ildiko after each session.

"I look forward to that day," Raysel replied. His brows furrowed together at the sight of the welt already rising on her arm, and he began to sort through the jars looking for the right one to use.

"It feels good outside tonight. Why don't we eat by the waterfall?" Nerissa suggested as Raysel slathered the salve onto her upper arm. It produced a sensation that was simultaneously soothing and cooling.

"That sounds like a good idea," Raysel agreed. He followed up the salve with a generous application of a clear gel that smelled so pungent it made Nerissa's eyes water and then finished by wrapping the area in gauze. "Where else are you hurt?"

Nerissa held out her left hand, where her palm and thumb were already puffy and swollen, and Raysel set about dutifully applying the salve.

———————◆———————

A little while later, two pairs of sandals sat in a jumble at the base of Raysel's favorite tree by the waterfall. Not far above them, among the leaves tinged red and yellow, dangled four bare feet. The aroma of food wafted through the air, mixing with the mossy scent of running water. The moon, now three-quarters full, illuminated the boxed dinners that Raysel and Nerissa held on their laps.

Nerissa smiled with pleasure as she took a bite of her chicken. The sauce, made with lemon and orange zest, was refreshing after a long day of training. The salve Raysel put on her arm earlier had a numbing effect, so while the pain was still there, it was dulled sufficiently enough that she could enjoy her food.

"Ildiko never fails to make delicious meals," Raysel said before stuffing a forkful of herbed rice into his mouth.

Nerissa snatched up the last piece of chicken. "I've eaten a lot of good food, and Ildiko's cooking is definitely among the best," she agreed. She swung her feet contentedly and gingerly leaned back onto the branch behind them.

The peaceful stillness was interrupted by a sudden yell— an unintelligible whooping—followed by a loud splash as something large hit the water. Not even a second later, an identical call echoed through the trees and another pale mass vaulted into the pond.

Nerissa blinked, trying to process what she had just seen. Those two men had appeared to be completely… She shook her head in denial. No, surely they wouldn't have been.

A moment later, her suspicions were confirmed when Raysel yelled out, "Put some clothes on, you two! You're not the only ones here, and I shouldn't see a full moon for a few more days!"

Nerissa stared down at the empty tray of food in her lap,

studiously avoiding looking up at the pond again.

"You're ruining our appetite too!" Raysel added.

Two heads bobbed up and down in the water as the pair swam toward Raysel and Nerissa. "It's too hot for clothes tonight!" one called back.

"What's the harm? There aren't any women around anyway," the second one chimed in.

Raysel squeezed Nerissa's good shoulder comfortingly, and she laid her hand on top of his. "It's fine; he's right. As far as he knows at least," she murmured.

"It doesn't matter," Raysel replied. "I don't particularly enjoy the sight of their bare bottoms either." He slid his tray into his bag and hopped down from the tree as the two swimmers neared the shore in front of them.

"Is that you, Raysel?" one asked.

"Oh, the new guy is here too!" the second one said when Nerissa dropped down beside Raysel. He stood, having reached the shallow edge of the pond, and walked toward them.

Nerissa's eyes widened at the sight of him, and she tore her gaze away to stare fixedly up at the sky.

"For the last time, get back in the water! Neither one of us wants to see you naked!" Raysel said, exasperated.

"I was going to introduce myself to Caeneus," the first one complained, jumping back into the water with a splash.

"That's not exactly the proper way to introduce yourself, brother," the second one scolded. He turned back to Nerissa and Raysel. "It's alright, he's decent enough again."

"Sorry, I wasn't thinking," the first one said sheepishly. He knocked on his skull and laughed. "It's totally hollow sometimes."

"His might be, but mine isn't," the second one said.

Raysel sighed. "Caeneus, meet Cole and Eloc," he said, gesturing to the pair, who were now standing in chest-height water.

They waved back simultaneously and called out "Hello!" in eerie unison.

"Good luck figuring out which one is which. No one in Darnal can tell for sure," Raysel said.

"Not even our mother," the first twin chimed merrily. "And that's how we like it."

"He's Cole and I'm Eloc," the second twin said. "If you're ever in doubt, Cole is the one with the hollow noggin."

Cole huffed and folded his arms across his chest. "You shouldn't be giving away our secrets," he said, now pouting and sticking his tongue out at his brother.

"Believe it or not, these two both specialize in hand-to-hand combat, but that isn't their most valuable talent. Their family is known for being expert disguise specialists," Raysel explained.

"We can be anybody we want to be," Eloc boasted.

"Even women!" Cole added.

Nerissa's brows rose. That was quite an impressive—and useful—talent indeed. "Seems you two are more than just a couple of skinny-dipping goofballs."

They both guffawed. "Oh, I like this new guy!" Cole said.

"We work hard all day, so we deserve to have fun at night," Eloc replied. "Want to swing off the rope with us?" he asked, pointing at a rope that dangled from a tree limb on the opposite side of the pond.

"I-I-I'll pass," Nerissa stammered.

"It's time for us to head back," Raysel told the twins.

"We'll be off then," Cole said.

"It was nice meeting you. See you around!" Eloc added.

They turned at the same time and dove under the water. Two pairs of bare bottoms briefly popped above the surface before disappearing completely.

At that sight, Nerissa spun away again. "Are all men that, ah, comfortable around one another?" she asked Raysel.

He rubbed his forehead and laughed uneasily. "No, those two are a special case. I hope they didn't shock you too much."

"I was surprised. It's not that I haven't seen such a thing before," she fibbed.

Raysel gave her a sideways glance, one eyebrow raised. "That's a surprise. You never showed a bit of interest in any of your noble suitors that I'm aware of."

Nerissa flushed crimson all the way to her ears. "You make it sound like I'm a prude, but you're right," she admitted. "I have definitely lived a sheltered life until now. I suppose in the future 'Caeneus' should not be quite as flustered as I am."

"I don't think you'll have too much to worry about. Those two are..." he paused, searching for the right word, "unique in many ways." He reached up to fetch his bag from the branches. "Let's hurry back," he said as a splash and riotous laughter echoed behind them.

Nerissa couldn't agree more.

---

Based on the number of shoes in the entryway of Einar and Ildiko's home, it seemed that there were visitors. Nerissa followed Raysel into the kitchen where Haku, Hania, and Einar were seated around the table. The conversation paused as they entered, then continued after Einar motioned for the two to join them at the table.

Ildiko nodded to the pair from where she stood drying dishes at the countertop island, and Raysel passed the table to return their empty dinner boxes to her. He quietly thanked her for the delicious meal and then pulled a chair over to take a seat beside Nerissa. They both remained silent, waiting to be addressed first.

"I agree that the twins would be a good choice for this mission," Einar said. "A group of all men would be more conspicuous to any Senka present compared to a group of men and women."

"Yes, the twins' ability to disguise themselves as females would be advantageous in this situation," Haku replied.

Hania propped his chin on his fist and addressed Raysel and Nerissa. "We are preparing a mission," he said. "Raysel, you will be the lead."

"What is our objective?" Raysel asked.

"My informant, Erik, has been monitoring the movements of a woman in his village for several months now.

The woman, Shae, earns a living as a plant oil purifier but is also a renowned prophetess. Queen Echidna was seen visiting her home the day before Casimer's attack. Just hours prior to Echidna's visit, Shae sent a message containing a—supposedly—prophetic warning about the impending attack. It is unclear whether or not she had contact with the Queen before sending it," Hania explained.

Nerissa's eyes widened. She had heard mention of Erik's observations several times now in reports from Hania but had been unaware of the direct connection to the attack until now. Beside her, Raysel curled and uncurled his fists, listening intently.

"You think it's possible Shae may have had prior knowledge of the attack and sent the message under the guise of a prophecy?" Raysel asked. He stilled his hands, but Nerissa could feel the floor vibrating slightly as he tapped his foot near hers beneath the table.

"We can't rule that out," Haku replied. "Shae and Echidna could have conspired to use the message as a ruse to get Erik out of the village before the Queen's visit."

"That would be very troubling. If it's true, Erik's role as our informant has been compromised," Raysel said slowly.

"That is one possibility," Einar answered. "On the other hand, she may have known ahead of time and betrayed Echidna by sending the warning. Or the prophecy could truly have been genuine. We haven't yet determined where Shae's loyalties lie."

Raysel nodded solemnly. "Has she had continued contact with Echidna?"

"Not that we are aware of," Hania said. "However, several new pieces of information have recently come to light. Erik's wife overheard a conversation between Shae and her daughter. The two of them were talking about going to the University Library to search for a book containing an ancient prophecy about Casimer."

Nerissa inhaled sharply. Erik's wife must be quite an accomplished spy to have been able to obtain such detailed information.

"Is this prophecy a message of some sort to help Casimer?" Raysel asked.

"Unfortunately, we don't know anything more about the nature of the prophecy," Einar grumbled.

"What we *do* know is that Shae and her daughter are planning to visit Niamh for the Fall Arts Festival at the University. According to Erik, neither of them has ever been outside the village. Their sudden decision to attend the festival has to be related to their search for the book."

Nerissa's thoughts immediately flew to Charis. Her friend seemed to know every book the University Library held. "Perhaps Charis would be of assistance to us in finding the book."

"Her knowledge may have been helpful under different circumstances," Einar said. "But there is a further complication. Casimer's nephew, Amon, is a close contact of hers. He has been studying at the University for the last year."

"I know him," Nerissa said.

"It is possible that Amon is not merely there to study and instead is there acting as an agent to uncover information under Casimer's orders."

Nerissa exhaled and leaned back into her chair. She knew Amon—and liked him—despite Charis' distrust of him. Perhaps her friend's suspicions were not misplaced.

"If Charis became involved, it could put her in a potentially dangerous situation," Einar concluded.

Nerissa gripped her knees beneath the table. "I do not want her to be put in danger."

"Then it is best that we not contact her for assistance," Hania said. "We believe that if we observe the pair long enough, we should be able to figure out exactly what their intentions are. Our plan is to send a group into Niamh to attend the Arts Festival and shadow Shae and her daughter. During that time, we will attempt to determine what book they are looking for. We may also be able to establish whether or not they have any involvement with Amon. If necessary, we will intercept them to prevent the information from getting into Casimer's hands."

"I understand," Raysel said. "Who will be included in the mission?"

"As I mentioned earlier, you will be the lead," Hania replied. "Cole and Eloc will accompany you in female disguise. Leal and Jarold will be assigned as well. Two of you will act as 'escorts' for Cole and Eloc, and the other will pose as a servant in order to move freely behind the scenes. You can decide the assignments as you see fit."

"I will be going as well," Nerissa declared, jumping in before Raysel could reply.

"Absolutely not!" Einar argued. "Your face is well known

throughout Niamh. The risk of someone recognizing you is far too great."

Nerissa spluttered, but she couldn't argue with his logic.

"That should be no problem if the twins give her a disguise in addition to her current guise as Caeneus," Raysel suggested. Nerissa squeezed his knee under the table gratefully.

"This mission is far too important for me not to be involved," Nerissa added.

The three chiefs traded glances with one another. Behind them, Ildiko smiled enigmatically and winked at Nerissa. Einar sighed and said, "Her safety will be your responsibility, Raysel."

"That's exactly what we've been training for," he replied, meeting Nerissa's eyes confidently.

"Very well," Haku said. "We will inform the other party members of their assignment in the morning. You will depart for Niamh in twelve days and arrive the day before the Festival."

Haku continued giving details in preparation for the mission while butterflies stirred in Nerissa's stomach as the ramifications of these new developments sank in. What was the nature of this prophecy? How was it related to a book at the University Library and which book could it be? There were thousands in the collection. The one they sought must be quite old, so it was likely a part of the library's Special Collection.

Nerissa didn't know a lot about Casimer, but she had learned a few basic things about him from her parents. He didn't seem to be the type of man who would give credibility to prophecies, so they must still be missing some important detail. Nerissa grasped her stomach, and the fluttering increased in intensity as she came to another realization.

If the book and the prophecy were as important as Erik's report made it sound, then a great deal of harm could be done if it fell into the wrong hands. Somehow, they would have to be sure to find it before anyone else did.

# LIST OF CHARACTERS

MAY CONTAIN SPOILERS

## Nerissa's Family and Friends

Addy—Pan's wife

Charis—Nerissa's best friend

Dallin—Childhood friend of Nerissa

Nerissa–Heiress of Chiyo

Pan—Baker in Niamh

Parlen—Nerissa's father, Bond of Chiyo

Rica—Nerissa's mother, Blood of Chiyo

Tao—Nerissa's mentor, teacher, researcher of crystals and their uses


## Casimer's family

Amon—Casimer's nephew

Casimer—King of Marise

Echidna—Queen of Marise

Ladon—Prince of Marise


## Ohanzee

Alala—Senka defector that takes refuge in Darnal, friend of Caelan

Aravind—Daughter of Haku and Ebba, apprentice blacksmith

Beadurinc—Personal guardian of Parlen and Rica

Caelan—Senka defector that takes refuge in Darnal, Rian's mother, teacher

Caeneus—Mysterious young man brought to Darnal by Einar

Cattleya—Daughter of Haku and Ebba, jewelry designer

Cole—Disguise specialist, twin of Eloc

Ebba—Wife of Haku, blacksmith

Einar—Nerissa's archery instructor, Chief Guardian

Eloc—Disguise specialist, twin of Cole

Gerda—Wife of Hania

Haku—Chief Preceptor

Hania—Chief Advisor

Harbin—Personal guardian of Parlen and Rica

Ildiko—Wife of Einar, practitioner of medicine

Jarold—Swordsman and hand-to-hand combat specialist

Leal—Swordsman

Raysel—Son of Haku and Ebba, First Swordsman of the Ohanzee, Nerissa's personal guardian

Rian—Swordsman, Raysel's best friend

Valter—Personal guardian of Parlen and Rica


## Senka

Nils—Chief of the Senka


## Others

Akkub—Governor of Silvus

Alden—Governor of Rhea

Argia—Prophetess during the time of King Gared

Darci—Daughter of Akkub

Desta—Daughter of Shae

Erik—Village messenger, Ohanzee agent

King Gared—First King of Renatus, united the land after the Fall of Civilization

Gladys—Wife of Erik

Gullintanni—Secret group that defends Renatus under orders of King Gared

Luca—Valen's mentor

Shae—Prophetess, extractor of plant oils

Valen—Argia's guide


## Lands and Towns

Chiyo—Country ruled by Rica and Parlen

Darnal—Hidden city of the Ohanzee

Marise—Country ruled by Casimer and Echidna

Maze—City in Marise with network of underground canals

Niamh—Capital of Chiyo

Nyx—Capital of Marise

Renatus—Name encompassing all the lands of the world

Rhea—Capital city of the mountain province of Rhea

Silvus—Capital city of the province of Silvus

Yoshie River—River that borders Rhea on three sides

## ABOUT THE AUTHOR

Rachel R. Smith lives near Cincinnati, Ohio with her husband and the cutest dog in the world, Sumo. When not writing, she plots to fill the interior of their home with books and mineral specimens and to cover the exterior with roses. Stay up to date on the series and learn more about Rachel by visiting her blog at http://www.recordsoftheohanzee.com or by following Records of the Ohanzee on Facebook (RecordsOfTheOhanzee) and Instagram (@rachel_r._smith).

## WORKS BY RACHEL R. SMITH

*Reflection: The Stranger in the Mirror*

*Reflection: Harbinger of the Phoenix*

*Reflection: Thorn of the White Rose*

*Reflection: Dragon's Bane*

*Revenant: The Undead King*
(Records of the Ohanzee Book 5, Forthcoming)

Made in the USA
San Bernardino, CA
24 February 2018